"When we face great pain or loss, these are the times when we may be tempted to ask whether God's care is reliable. And it is especially in times like these when Jesus speaks from the place of his cross. He empathizes with us and is present to help. In *Remember Me*, Sharon tells a compelling and grace-rich story that helps us enter into these realities. I was touched and helped as I read. I believe you will be, too."

Alan Fadling, author of *An Unhurried Life*, founder and president of Unhurried Living

"I've already read *Remember Me* more than once, and as with all of Sharon Garlough Brown's novels, I'll savor it again. Through her true-to-life characters and powerful story, she interweaves themes of suffering, lament, and mental health with beauty, hope, and resurrection. When I finished it, my faith in our living, loving God was strengthened and renewed."

Amy Boucher Pye, author of *The Living Cross*

"If the literary world had a spiritual director, Sharon Garlough Brown would be it. Through the backdoor of the imagination, she encourages us to brave vulnerability in spiritual friendships and gently prods us toward a more robust vision of genuine community. I can think of no other living novelist doing this so consistently, with such wisdom, excellence, and patience."

Sarah Arthur, preliminary fiction judge of the Christianity Today Book Awards and author of *A Light So Lovely: The Spiritual Legacy of Madeleine L'Engle*

"Can the path of suffering and grief carry us to a place of healing as we journey to the cross? Author Sharon Garlough Brown's new book *Remember Me* offers a stunningly beautiful narrative of restoration and redemption in two women's lives. . . . I loved this tender telling of the slow dance into new life and highly recommend it for any season of sorrow, but especially during Lent. I'm grateful it includes a Stations of the Cross personal exercise. What a poignant reminder that new life will come as we persevere in seeking the Lord."

Lucinda Secrest McDowell, author *Life-Giving Choices* and *Ordinary Graces*

"Sharon Garlough Brown understands the powerful potential of letter writing and art to express deepest feelings. She lets one of the protagonists of her beautifully and sensitively written novel bare her soul, expose her grief, and affirm her deep faith to the young artist struggling with her own grief and faith and confidence in her artistic abilities. For both the writer of the letters and the receiver, this thoughtful way of communicating brings peace, resolution, and healing. *Remember Me* offers the reader a powerful tool of self-reflection and a safe and intimate way to explore the depths of the soul—through letter-journaling as well as through the expressive language of art."

Carol A. Berry, author of *Learning from Henri Nouwen and Vincent Van Gogh: A Portrait of the Compassionate Life*

"One of the deepest human longings is the longing to be understood—and there are few experiences in life when this ache surfaces more urgently than in the throes of depression and grief. In *Remember Me*, Sharon Garlough Brown vividly illuminates what it's like to be engulfed in depression's shadow and isolated by its despair. She puts words to what many of us have experienced but lack a vocabulary to describe. Through the sometimes tentative yet always tender support given by Kit to Wren, Brown illustrates what it looks like to heal in and through relationship. This novella is unquestionably written for those longing to be understood and those seeking to understand the desolate experience of mental illness."

Beth A. Booram, cofounder and director of Fall Creek Abbey, coauthor of *When Faith Becomes Sight*

"*Remember Me*, Sharon Garlough Brown's sequel to *Shades of Light*, is a novella filled with heartbreaking beauty and profound truth. Readers will savor this story as they join Kit and Wren on a Lenten journey contemplating the stations of the cross. Kit's letters to Wren, grace filled and laced with deep sorrow from her own trauma and heartbreak, show how Christ uses 'companions in sorrow' to come alongside those who are grieving. There are no easy answers here, but the reader is invited to sit with both Kit and Wren in the not knowing, not having the answers they hoped for, not having one kind of closure but finding closure in a better way. The artwork and reflection questions add yet another dimension to this potentially life-changing message. I found great hope and freedom in this story."

Elizabeth Musser, author of *When I Close My Eyes*

"Most of us find grief and waiting to be two of the most challenging aspects of life. With the skillful precision of a spiritual director, Sharon Garlough Brown connects us with engaging characters who are working through deep loss. *Remember Me* offers hope in the midst of waiting and empathy in the midst of grief. Thank you, Sharon, for leading us straight to the cross, where we find a suffering Christ, ready to meet us."

Gem Fadling, author of *What Does Your Soul Love?* and founder of Unhurried Living

Remember Me

A NOVELLA ABOUT FINDING OUR WAY TO THE CROSS

SHARON GARLOUGH BROWN

ivp

An imprint of InterVarsity Press
Downers Grove, Illinois

InterVarsity Press
P.O. Box 1400, Downers Grove, IL 60515-1426
ivpress.com
email@ivpress.com

InterVarsity Press® is the book-publishing division of InterVarsity Christian Fellowship/USA®, a movement of students and faculty active on campus at hundreds of universities, colleges, and schools of nursing in the United States of America, and a member movement of the International Fellowship of Evangelical Students. For information about local and regional activities, visit intervarsity.org.

Scripture quotations, unless otherwise noted, are from the New Revised Standard Version of the Bible, copyright 1989 by the Division of Christian Education of the National Council of the Churches of Christ in the USA. Used by permission. All rights reserved.

This is a work of fiction. People, places, events, and situations are either the product of the author's imagination or are used fictitiously. Any resemblance to events, locales, or actual persons, living or dead, is entirely coincidental.

Sharon Garlough Brown, Awakened, used courtesy of the author.

Sharon Garlough Brown and Elizabeth Ivy Hawkins, Lament (sorrow collage), used courtesy of the artists. "Window Light" and "Fallen Heart Leaf" photos used courtesy of Therese Kay Photography.

Bette Lynn Dickinson, "It Is Finished," panel of the work What Breathes Beneath Our Story, used courtesy of Bette Lynn Dickinson. www.bettedickinson.life

Elizabeth Ivy Hawkins, Pressed, Handed Over, From the Ashes, Remember Me, Hope Rises, and plate and cup charcoal sketch, used by permission. www.elizabethivy.com

Cover design and image composite: David Fassett
Interior design: Jeanna Wiggins
Cover images: hand-painted cross: © Olga Kashurina / iStock / Getty Images Plus
    pastel shades on textured surface: © andipantz / iStock / Getty Images Plus
    red paint brush stroke: © R.Tsubin / Moment Collection / Getty Images
    painted texture: © Sergey Ryumin / Moment Collection / Getty Images

ISBN 978-0-8308-4670-2 (print)
ISBN 978-0-8308-4832-4 (digital)

Printed in the United States of America ♾

Library of Congress Cataloging-in-Publication Data

Names: Brown, Sharon Garlough, author.
Title: Remember me : a novella about finding our way to the cross / Sharon Garlough Brown.
Description: Downers Grove, Illinois : IVP, an imprint of InterVarsity Press, [2019]
Identifiers: LCCN 2019041580 (print) | LCCN 2019041581 (ebook) | ISBN 9780830846702 (print ; alk. paper) | ISBN 9780830848324 (digital)
Subjects: GSAFD: Christian fiction.
Classification: LCC PS3602.R722867 R46 2019 (print) | LCC PS3602.R722867 (ebook) | DDC 813/.6—dc23
LC record available at https://lccn.loc.gov/2019041580
LC ebook record available at https://lccn.loc.gov/2019041581

P	21	20	19	18	17	16	15	14	13	12	11	10	9	8	7	6	5	4	3	2
Y	37	36	35	34	33	32	31	30	29	28	27	26	25	24	23	22	21	20		

For my beloved dad,

CLARENCE M. GARLOUGH,

who fought the good fight and finished his race
a few months after I finished writing this book.

His kindness, love, and faithfulness helped me trust the
kindness, love, and faithfulness of my heavenly Father.

Thank you, Dad. You're my hero, and I love you.

No eye has seen, nor ear heard, nor human heart conceived,
what God has prepared for those who love him.
(1 CORINTHIANS 2:9)

Contents

1

The Word Became Flesh

CHRISTMAS EVE

She was safe. Not well, not at peace, but safe.

Katherine Rhodes lingered in the bedroom doorway and offered a silent prayer for Wren, who was writhing and whimpering in her sleep, no doubt tormented by her usual nightmares over all she had been unable to prevent. *If she had been more attentive. If she had been more assertive. If she had recognized the signs and demanded Casey get help.*

Kit quietly shut the door. Not all the way, though. The three-inch gap was a psychological prop—even if it didn't provide physical protection. She had been unable to provide such protection for her son, and she would be unable to provide it for her great-niece.

If she had been more attentive, if she had been more assertive, if she had recognized the signs and demanded Micah get help, then maybe he would be in the prime of midlife instead of forever seventeen.

The same voices harassing Wren had plagued Kit for many years, and though she had long ago become practiced in recognizing their source and rejecting them, noticing and naming the voices didn't mean they went silent—just dormant, waiting to be awakened by some other crisis when she felt out of control and yet responsible.

She dialed Jamie's number as she descended the stairs. "She's okay. Just sleeping."

"I'm sorry to keep pestering you for updates," Jamie said, "but when I couldn't get her to answer her phone . . ."

"No, I know. I promise, I'll call you if I notice anything new." She had made that same promise to Jamie many times over the past couple of months, ever since offering her home as a place for Wren to regroup and recover after her stay at Glenwood Psychiatric Hospital. But a mother didn't outgrow anxiety, especially for an already fragile daughter now catapulted into the additional trauma of losing her closest friend not quite two weeks ago.

"I don't suppose she'll make it to church tonight." There was something wistful in Jamie's voice, as if a Christmas miracle were still a possibility.

"No, I don't think so. But her pastor is coming to see her between the services."

"Oh! That's good. I'm glad to hear that. Please thank her for me."

"I will." While Wren had accepted Hannah's invitation to bring her communion on Christmas Eve, she might not remember the conversation. Kit didn't want Wren to miss the opportunity to receive it, though. Receiving communion from elders who took turns visiting the house was one of the few things Kit vividly remembered from the days after Micah died. Robert didn't want to participate. She hadn't blamed him. Not for that, anyway. But when she'd felt so disconnected from her life, so disembodied with grief, chewing the bread and swallowing the juice was a tactile way to practice faith when she felt as if she didn't have any faith to practice.

Jamie said, "And what about tomorrow? Are you heading to Sarah's?"

"We'll play that by ear, see how Wren's feeling." Kit had already prepared her daughter for the possibility of not joining the family for their celebration. *The girls will be so disappointed,* Sarah had said, with a tone that communicated her own. But it couldn't be helped. Leaving Wren alone for an extended period simply wasn't safe.

"I can never thank you enough for all you've done, Kit, for all you're doing. I know I keep saying that, but I don't know what else to say."

"I'm glad to be able to do it." Kit paused on the bottom stair landing and peered through the beveled glass on the front door. The cul-de-sac was quiet. "I hope you and Dylan and the kids can have a wonderful celebration together, even with all this."

"I'm trying," Jamie said.

"I know you are. You're doing so well."

"Some days are better than others." Jamie sighed. "I've got to go get costumes ready for the nativity play. Joseph has the stomach flu, and none of the other boys is willing to play the role. So Phoebe has agreed to give up being a sheep and step in. Olivia is painting on a mascara beard and mustache as we speak."

Kit laughed. "Take pictures. Lots of them. And I'll ask Wren to call you later if she's up to it."

As she waited for Hannah to arrive, Kit debated whether she should try to wrap the two Vincent van Gogh prints she'd purchased for Wren: *Starry Night* and *Olive Trees*. Opening wrapping paper might require too much effort. Or stir painful memories of other Christmas celebrations. Maybe it was best simply to give her the prints without making note of them being Christmas gifts.

She sat on the sofa, the prints side by side on her lap, and thought about the many conversations she and Wren had shared about Vincent's life and faith, about how some of his work evoked images of Jesus wrestling in Gethsemane and how they hoped to partner together in creating content and art for the Journey to the Cross at New Hope.

But that was before Casey died. Given Wren's current state of mind, it was unlikely she would be able to meditate on the Scriptures, let alone paint a prayerful response to them in time for Holy Week. And as far as weaving her own story into the New Hope reflections—as Kit had told Wren she would consider doing—the more she thought about it, the more she realized that wasn't the right context. People who came to New Hope for the Journey to the Cross came to pray with the Word and the art, not to read someone's personal narrative.

Still, Wren had bravely asked her to share her story. And though no words of wisdom or consolation, no words about the loss of her son or her own journey with depression could mitigate Wren's suffering in these early days of her anguish, perhaps there was another way to offer Wren what she'd asked for.

If she told her story in small doses, wrapping bits of personal narrative around the Journey to the Cross Scripture texts, then Wren could read it when she was well enough to process it. And return to it whenever she needed to be reminded that she was not alone. "Companions in misfortune," Wren often said, quoting Vincent. As much as she loved reading his letters to his brother, maybe she would appreciate reading letters written to her.

Kit glanced over her shoulder at headlights in the driveway and set the prints aside. Considering the ways Wren's journey had already tapped her own subterranean sorrow, she suspected that by saying yes to writing letters, she might be saying yes to much more.

With the cross casting its shadow on the manger, tonight was as good a time as any to begin.

CHRISTMAS EVE

My dear Wren,

Tonight I watched your pastor offer you a bit of bread and hold the cup to your lips so you could drink. "Do this and remember me," she said. You chewed and swallowed, then sank back into your bed to sleep.

I know you can't remember much right now. Grief has carved too deep a chasm. So we trust the even deeper mysteries and receive by faith what we cannot receive through reason or effort. We receive Christ's death and life in our places of death and wait. And when we cannot wait with hope, we let others practice hope for us.

A few weeks ago you asked if I ever share my story at the retreats I lead at New Hope. I told you that I haven't because I've never wanted the content to point to me. If our suffering has been severe, our testimonies can become a distraction or even a stumbling block to those who might be reluctant to grieve their own losses, especially if they're tempted to talk themselves out of their pain by measuring it against or comparing it with someone else's. There are no star sufferers, however, in the kingdom of God. So, as I share from my own story, I pray my words won't shine a spotlight on me but reveal instead how Jesus has met me in the losses and enlarged me through them. That's my hope for you, too, that the excruciating pain you have endured and that you're enduring right now will become a pathway toward deeper communion with the One who is with you in it.

Even as I begin, I'm mindful that we are unreliable narrators of our own stories. But who else can tell them from the inside? Some of my memories are only recollections of what others told me I said I was thinking or feeling when I was in the depths of despair. I'll try to offer you the same gift, to hold the things you cannot hold right now but might want to remember later. And if I record details you wish you could forget, please forgive me.

Tonight I'll light my Christ candle and, for both of us, I'll rehearse the truth that is a comfort to me in times like these, that the Word became flesh and dwelt among us. We have seen his glory, even if only in a mirror darkly. Jesus, in offering his bruised and wounded flesh—in giving his body broken for us—makes us whole, even when it doesn't seem like wholeness. This, we receive by faith. Tonight, for both of us, I'll also rehearse the truth that is hard to receive and trust in times like these, that the light shines in the darkness, and the darkness will never overcome it.

I'm keeping watch with you, dear one.

Love,

Kit

2

The Gift of Myrrh

EPIPHANY

She and Robert had argued in an office lobby similar to the one where she now waited for Wren to finish her counseling appointment. Kit had asked him to lower his voice—*please*—especially in front of other patients. They could speak to the counselor privately about what kind of addiction treatment programs might be most helpful for their son. But Robert had heard of such programs, and it was a waste of money, he said. Perfectly normal for teenagers to experiment. He had experimented when he was Micah's age and hadn't suffered any long-term detriment. She was hovering and controlling, Robert said, and maybe if she weren't so judgmental and condemning—maybe if she would just back off and give Micah space to figure things out, and yes, fail if he needed to, why did she think she could prevent that?—he would outgrow this rebellious phase, just as Robert had.

There was no arguing her husband out of his position, especially when the counselor "took her side" and agreed that more aggressive treatment, which could also help address Micah's underlying depression, would be a prudent course of action. Robert refused to meet with the counselor again, and his disparaging remarks about therapy in general and Micah's therapist in particular—which he routinely made in front of their son—severed Micah's already tenuous commitment to his appointments. Kit couldn't force him to go. She'd tried and failed.

Wren, thankfully, did not object to going to her appointments, and her counselor had wisely set multiple dates in advance so Wren wouldn't have to exert herself in making phone calls. All Kit needed to do was remind her when it was time to go and drive her there. And reassure Jamie that yes, Wren was meeting with Dawn. Jamie had learned not to press for specifics, much as she longed for them. Kit understood the longing. And the fear.

She flipped through a magazine, looking at photos. On their way out, she would ask the receptionist if she could have some of the outdated ones to cut up for prayer collages for the retreat session that night. Wren would need to go with her to New Hope so she wouldn't be alone at the house, and while Kit led the retreat, Wren would probably sleep in one of the guestrooms. Not the one where Casey was supposed to stay, though. Kit had closed and locked that door, thinking it would be better for her if she couldn't access that space. But sometimes Kit found her in the chapel, resting her head on the chair where he had left his goodbye letter. Vincent had painted a friend's empty chair, Wren had said in one of her more lucid moments. Empty chairs made her cry.

Kit let her mind drift to their old kitchen table, Micah's chair pulled out at precisely the angle he had left it. At least, she thought it was the way he'd left it. There had been no memorable last supper together, only an ordinary dinner with their forks scraping against their plates, the sound amplified by the absence of conversation. If she had known she would find her beloved boy the next morning, cold in his bed, what last words would she have tried to speak to him? What words would she have begged him to speak to her?

At least Wren had Casey's handwritten note—his intentions a mystery, yes, but his love and regret unmistakable. That was a gift.

Dawn's office door opened and Wren emerged, her dark, unwashed hair partially covered by Casey's beanie. If Kit could persuade her to relinquish the hat for an hour, she could wash it for her. Wren probably wasn't aware of the odor emanating from her clothes or body. She hardly had energy to change a shirt, let alone shower, poor thing.

"I'll see you next week," Dawn said, her hand resting on Wren's shoulder. If Wren replied, audibly or otherwise, Kit missed it. But for a moment her own gaze met Dawn's, and Dawn acknowledged her with a nod, as if to say, "Thank you" and "Please keep doing what you're doing."

Kit set the magazine down on the end table. She had enough prayer collage photos to choose from. She would ask for extras another time.

"It won't take me long to get things organized," she said as they drove to New Hope. "Then we can head home for a rest before we come back for the retreat." Straightforward and brief declarations rather than questions seemed to work best. Asking Wren what she felt well enough to do or giving her options only overwhelmed her.

Kit glanced toward the passenger seat, where Wren was leaning her head against the window, eyes closed. The therapy appointments, as necessary as they were, probably exhausted her. Kit remembered nothing from her counseling appointments after Micah died, only that Robert drove her because she didn't trust herself behind the wheel of a car. He drove her to the psychiatric hospital too, after her counselor insisted she needed inpatient treatment. Kit hadn't had the energy to object, not to the therapist or Robert, who carried in her suitcase after her intake exam. Odd, how some images were indelibly branded into memory while others left no imprint. He'd set the burgundy case on the green paisley carpet, kissed her on the cheek, and said he'd call the hospital later to check on her. He kept his word. About that, he did.

At New Hope she parked in front of the lobby entrance and opened the car door for Wren when she gave no sign of exiting. "There you go," Kit said as she reached for her hand, "watch your step here. That's it. We'll just check in with Gayle and see what else needs to be done to get ready." A few weeks ago Wren would have been the one scrubbing bathrooms, vacuuming hallways, and tidying the chapel. Now if she managed to use a duster, it was a victory. Thankfully, Gayle, the part-time receptionist, was willing to put in extra hours to help. She was sympathetic: she had an adult daughter who suffered from depression.

After greeting both of them warmly, Gayle handed Kit a registration list and a few file folders. "I've pulled out some of the photo categories I thought might be helpful for the collages."

Kit thumbed through the labels: food, architecture, nature. These were probably Gayle's own preferences. "Let's add the 'hands and feet' and 'roads and pathways' files too," Kit said, "for variety's sake." She paused, trying to discern her next move, then decided to tread lightly. "Here—let's ask the artist, shall we?" She lightly touched Wren's coat sleeve to try to draw her in. "Wren's done these collages before and has a good eye for such things. Let's set the folders down on the table here and take a look." Kit went to the file cabinet and removed the rest of them. "There's an 'art' one here—I forgot I had that one. And an 'objects' one and a 'people and faces' one." She set the manila folders next to one another without opening them. "Let's take a look here, Wren. Just the titles. And you give me a yay or nay. What's good for a New Year theme? Art?"

She watched Wren for any response. After a few long moments of silence, Wren nodded.

"Okay, good," Kit said. "What about food?"

Her response was marginally quicker—a slight shake of the head. Not surprising. Ever since Casey died, Kit hadn't found much food that enticed her. "Okay, we'll set this one aside for now. But this one is kind of interesting, the 'hands and feet' one. Would you like to take a look and see what you think?"

To Kit's delight, Wren reached forward and opened the file herself. After a moment's silence, she murmured, "Yes."

Such a good word, *yes*. "Right. And what about one more? How about if you choose between the 'roads and pathways' and 'people and faces'?"

Wren hesitated, then said quietly, "You could put all of them out."

Kit smiled. "Well, you're right about that. There's no reason not to, is there? Let people choose from a wide variety of what speaks to them. Good idea." She gathered the file folders together and nudged Wren's shoulder gently. "Maybe even the food one, huh? Someone might like to choose a cake or plum or something."

Wren nodded again. Kit handed her the folders. "I'll get the glue sticks and cardstock squares, if you can carry these folders down to the big classroom for me and set them on the table. We can either leave the folders for people to browse through, or we can pull out some photos for them to select from. Could you do that for me, Wren? Carry those to the room?"

"Okay."

"Great. I'll be there in a minute." After Wren disappeared around the corner, Kit thanked Gayle.

"Sure thing." Gayle lowered her voice. "She seems a little brighter today, don't you think?"

"Maybe a bit."

It was a temptation she would need to fight, Kit thought as she walked down the hallway a few minutes later—the temptation to monitor Wren moment by moment for signs of improvement. It was something she had cautioned Jamie about as well, how it was more important to look for a larger trajectory toward wellness than at the daily questions of, "Did she eat? Did she shower? Did she change her clothes? Did she get out of bed? Did she engage in any conversation?" Not that those activities wouldn't be significant vital signs. But they couldn't become a basis for hope. Only

Christ crucified and risen could bear the weight of human hope. All other things would crumble under it. All earthly things, it seemed, did.

When Kit entered the large retreat space, Wren was at the center table, hovering over a jumbled mass of images, as if she had dumped out all the folders to swirl the pictures together. No matter. Kit could sort them again afterward. "Finding anything interesting?"

Wren gripped the top of her beanie with both hands and leaned closer to the table. Then she picked up a single scrap of paper, crumpled it, and stuffed it into her sweatpants pocket while murmuring something.

"What did you say, dear one?" Kit moved toward her, so she could hear if she replied.

"Too sad," Wren said.

Kit scanned the table, wondering what had provoked her. "Yes, I suppose some of them are, aren't they?" She reached for a photo of an elderly couple sitting on a park bench, feeding the birds. "Even the ones that look happy can be sad, can't they?" Especially if they portrayed broken dreams or unfulfilled longings. "We could make prayer collages sometime of all sad things, if you'd like."

Wren turned toward her, her large brown eyes dull and tired. Then she reached into her pocket, uncrumpled the photo, and handed it to Kit.

"Yes," Kit said quietly, "I see what you mean. That's very sad." With a deep breath, she handed back to Wren the photo of a young father cradling a sleeping infant close to his heart.

JANUARY 6

My dear Wren,

I had planned to lead the retreat group last night in prayerful reflection about new beginnings. But the time with you at the table yesterday, looking at pictures that mirrored our sorrow, inspired a different idea. So instead, I invited the group to choose images that reflected gifts they have longed for and received—or haven't received. I asked them, too, to choose images of things they have received that they wished they hadn't been given. It was a rich and meaningful time of communion as they shared the stories behind the images that stirred them.

As I thought about what I would have put in my own collage, here's what came to mind: a smiling couple on their wedding day, a pair of baby shoes, a high school graduation, an elderly woman sitting beside her husband on a park bench, and, like you, a young dad holding a baby.

Retrospect can be a gift, enabling us to see with gratitude what we may have missed the first time around. It can also be a burden, coloring otherwise happy occasions with the grief of losses we experience afterward. Like a wedding day photo of a couple deeply in love, having no reason to believe their love would not endure, having no inkling of the sorrows or trials that would devastate them even as they pledged "for better and for worse" to one another. Or that first pair of shoes purchased for a baby ready to take his first steps into the world. The parents coo and cheer those steps of freedom and independence, never thinking about the steps the child may take that lead toward suffering. It's a blessing for these moments not to be tainted by shadows of what may be, but to be fully savored as the good and generous gifts they are, given to us by a good and generous God.

As my beloved granddaughters took their first steps, I watched with a bittersweet joy I could not reveal to my daughter. I didn't want to taint

Sarah's experience of unadulterated delight. The girls will have their own journeys to make, and I watch and pray and long for them, even as I know I have no control over where their paths will lead. This is right and good and also hard. We are created in the image of a God who loves us too much to control us and who gives us freedom to choose even the paths that lead away from him. What a great and mysterious love. And also hard.

As you already know, my marriage did not survive the devastation of Micah's death. This is not to say that Micah's death caused it to end. Robert and I had already experienced many fractures that hadn't been properly attended to. And though we divorced many years ago, and though it's been seven years now since Robert died, the sight of a couple growing old together, whether in a photo or in person, has the power to tap and churn my latent sorrow.

That's the thing about losses: they stretch in both directions, coloring the past and the future. It's not only the loss itself but all the losses that follow. I don't only grieve what I lost with Micah and Robert. I also grieve the things that will never be, because of losing them. We were never able to celebrate Micah's graduation from high school. I didn't get to see my son start a career or a family. Robert and I didn't grow old together. That's why I don't think we ever stop grieving what we lose. I don't say this to discourage you but to affirm your sorrow. The grieving changes. The manifestation of grieving evolves. Some losses are soothed and healed by the passage of time. Others leave gaps that are never filled. You will always miss Casey because you will always love your friend. Sorrow is the painful evidence of our love.

Today—Epiphany—is a good day for me to be thinking about gifts: the good ones and the hard ones. I've been thinking about the magi and how that group of pagan astrologers recognized in the heavens a sign that others missed, and they devoted themselves to following it, no matter what the cost. I've been pondering the particular gifts they brought to Jesus, each gift a prophetic declaration of who he is and what his mission would be.

Gold. That's a gift a poor family might have gratefully received as a fitting tribute for a king. Frankincense. That would have been a fitting offering to a god—a fragrant resin used in sacrifice. Both were appropriate gifts for the Son of God, born King of the Jews. But it's the last one that catches my attention, the gift of myrrh. Isaiah doesn't mention it when he prophesies about the gold and frankincense that faraway nations and kings will bring to worship the Lord. And I wonder what Mary must have thought when they presented this anointing oil, used to embalm the dead, to her boy. Did she recoil from the terror of it? Did she, like Peter when Jesus predicted his cross, declare, "Never! This shall never happen to you!" or did she say, not for the first time and probably not for the last, "Let it be to me according to your word"?

What do we do with our unwanted gifts of myrrh, when the fragrance of death and sorrow lingers and clings? I've come to see there is only one way to receive it: by remembering that Jesus received it first. And not just him, but also those who loved him. And in this, I find comfort.

With you,

Kit

3

Taking the Cup

JANUARY

When Hannah arrived at her regular time on Sunday afternoon, Kit greeted her with an embrace, her ears tuned to any sound of movement from Wren upstairs. But it was quiet. Not even the creak of a mattress to acknowledge the chime of the doorbell. "Come on in. I can put the kettle on if you've got time."

"Wish I did. But I've got to get back to the church for a funeral."

Kit hung her coat and scarf in the closet. "That's a long day for you."

"It is, but I'm taking tomorrow off." She followed Kit into the kitchen. "How's she doing?"

"About the same. I managed to coax her into eating some soup earlier, so that's a victory. For both of us."

Hannah opened her bag and removed her communion supplies. "Is she awake?"

"Last time I checked. I told her you were coming, so we can head upstairs."

When they reached her room, the bedroom door was open, and

Wren was sitting beneath her blanket clutching Casey's beanie to her chest, the Van Gogh prints Kit had given her at Christmas side by side on her lap.

Hannah greeted her and sat in the chair beside the bed. "I recognize one of those," she said, pointing to *Starry Night*. "What's the other one?"

Wren took a moment, then said, "*Olive Trees*."

"They're beautiful," Hannah said. "Is it okay if I move them out of the way so we don't spill anything on them?"

Wren murmured her okay and Hannah propped them up on the long bureau so they would be visible from the bed.

Kit pulled up a desk chair. If Wren was being deliberate about looking at Vincent's art again, that was encouraging. While Hannah poured grape juice into her carved olivewood chalice, Kit gazed at the paintings, each churning with emotion, and wondered if Wren was able to find comfort in them as she had before. Maybe her thoughts would return to Jesus in Gethsemane and the consolation she'd discovered when she considered the terror he had experienced there. "The stoic ones bug me," Wren had once confided, referring to the common artistic renderings of Jesus engulfed in soft light in the garden, serene and surrendered, eyes lifted heavenward. "There's nothing comforting in them."

Kit agreed. Show him writhing in anguish, pleading for the cup to be removed. Show the Word made flesh—the same Word that spoke everything into being—show the Word groaning words to the Father that would go unanswered. Show him sweating, crying, wrestling. And then—only then—show him yielding to the Father's plan.

"In the same way," Hannah was saying, "after supper he took the cup . . . "

He took the cup. These were the words Kit pondered while Wren opened her mouth like a small child to receive the bread Hannah placed on her tongue.

He took the cup. And he offered it to his friends to drink so that they might participate in the new covenant, sealed in his blood. He took the cup.

But he also asked the Father to take the cup. He begged the Father to take the cup of suffering, judgment, wrath, and affliction and remove it from him. In the end, Jesus would take this cup too. And he would drink it to the bottom.

She watched Hannah tip the cup to Wren's lips so she could drink. As Wren stared at Hannah while she sipped, something in her eyes—a poignant mixture of sorrow, trust, and a longing for hope—summoned an image from Kit's well of memories. "Take it," she'd said, holding the cup to Micah's lips. "You'll feel better." He had stared at her, his eyes a mixture of pain, trust, and yes, a longing for relief. And he drank it to the bottom.

"Katherine."

Kit was startled by the sound of her name and looked up to see Hannah holding out the bread and cup for her. "Do this and remember me."

Kit took the bread. She took the cup. But the remembering was a sword through her heart.

After Hannah left and Wren went back to sleep, Kit knelt in her study, searching through a stack of pictures she'd never put into albums. If the Holy Spirit was asking her to take the cup of remembering and drink it to the bottom, then she needed to see her son in one of his last photos.

These images too, she thought as she dug through the box, could make a fine collage of sorrow: Micah at his tenth birthday party, sitting with cake and balloons at a restaurant table with Sarah and one of her friends because his closest friend wasn't close enough, evidently, to be bothered to come; Micah sitting alone on the bench during a middle school basketball game, his uniform loose on his small frame, watching the larger boys skillfully maneuver along the court; Micah in a tuxedo, standing with Sarah and her prom date in a decorated auditorium, because the girl who had agreed to go with him had ditched him at the dance.

Would it have been so hard, Lord, to give him the gift of one friend?

She touched the face of her sad and lonely boy, then kept digging until she found the photo she was looking for: Micah in a leg cast, the white plaster bearing witness to his isolation, the few signatures, doodles, and "Get well" wishes scrawled by the hands of family members, not peers. She removed the picture from the box. If there were photos of that last Thanksgiving together, they had long ago been lost. Or maybe they had ended up in boxes Robert removed from their house after the divorce. It was his side of the family that always gathered together for the Thanksgiving Day meal and a game of football, even in snow. His sister would host the gathering at her house and pretend she hadn't instructed Dylan and Patrick, both a few years older than Micah, to include their cousin in their fun. On more than one occasion Kit had overheard them groan in protest.

But on that last Thanksgiving together, when Dylan and Patrick were home from college, they did invite Micah to play. He hadn't wanted to; Kit could tell. He would have been happier reading a book in a corner, out of everyone's way. But Robert and his nephews had pestered him—they needed one more player so the teams would be even—so Kit urged him to put his book away for a little while and join the fun. A bit of harmless fun.

But it wasn't harmless. One hard tackle from one of the neighbor boys led to one awful cracking sound, to one piercing howl, to one trip to the hospital to treat one compound fracture, to one leg in an immobilizing cast, to one dose of codeine. One, which led to another, which led to another. And when the liquid codeine stopped working, morphine worked fine. In the end it wasn't Micah's experimenting with illegal drugs that killed him. It was the legal ones.

And she had held the cup for him to drink.

JANUARY 14

My dear Wren,

I'm thinking tonight about cups—both the cups I have resisted and the cups I have drunk from. Watching you drink from Hannah's communion cup stirred many thoughts and feelings for me. I think it was the expression of trust and longing in your eyes as you drank, as if you truly wanted to believe that the words she offered you are true and that the presence of Christ is real. I saw sorrow. I saw weariness. But I also saw hope. I was grateful to see that glimmer again.

After you went to bed, I searched through old family photos for one of Micah, taken a few months before he died. I don't know how much your parents ever told you about Micah's death. It was fairly common knowledge that Micah died of a drug overdose, deemed accidental. That detail is a story for another time, I think. Enough to say that my son was sad and lonely. His counselor was trying to help him deal with his depression. But Micah began to self-medicate with marijuana and alcohol. I was concerned enough to try to get him into a residential treatment program. His father and I disagreed, though, and I lost the argument.

A few months later Micah was injured while playing football with Robert, your dad, and some cousins and neighbors. The doctor at the hospital prescribed painkillers for him. I made sure he took them regularly as prescribed. What I didn't realize is that he became dependent on them and that he started using them to medicate not only his physical pain but his emotional and mental pain too.

People typically assign blame when they hear "drug overdose," and especially with teenagers, people can wonder how parents can "let it happen." Believe me, I cast plenty of blame on myself for Micah's affliction. I also cast plenty of blame on God for not delivering him from it.

Tonight I felt led into remembering Micah in a way I haven't let myself do for a very long time. Drinking the cup of remembrance can be a painful experience, and we must go prayerfully at the Holy Spirit's bidding. As I drank that cup, another cup also appeared: the cup of guilt and regret. It's a bitter cup, Wren, full of poison. Nothing good can come from drinking it. It's a cup the Lord longs to remove from us.

I've heard you say it's your fault Casey died, that you didn't do enough or see enough or love enough. I felt the same way after I lost Micah. Maybe in the stupor of our sorrow we're so desperate to feel anything, we'll choose self-inflicted wounds of blame over the promise of comfort. Or the freedom of grace.

Tonight, instead of drinking that bitter cup to the dregs, I was able to remember that Jesus drank it for me. All my shame, all my guilt, all my failures—all of it was in the cup of affliction he willingly drank. He drank it so I wouldn't have to. So you wouldn't have to.

I guess I didn't realize I still had that cup. I'm grateful the Lord shined light on it. I'm asking him to take that cup away from you, even as I've asked him to take it away from me. Again.

With you,

Kit

4

With a Kiss

JANUARY

"Thanks for being willing to meet here today," Kit said to her spiritual director, Russell Groves, as she welcomed him into her office.

"Happy to."

As she prepared to close the door, she glanced down the hallway at the room where Wren was sleeping. If she woke and needed anything, Gayle was available to help. "Are you counting down the weeks?" Kit asked.

He sat down in the armchair, the brown vinyl squeaking beneath him. "Ginny is. She's already got the cruise booked." After decades of serving as a preaching professor at a local seminary, Russell was retiring in May. "It'll be an adjustment, not teaching, but I keep reminding myself I can always do adjunct work if I get bored. That is, if they'll have an old guy like me."

She smiled and moved aside a throw pillow before settling herself on the couch. "I'm sure they'd be happy to have you." She'd had the privilege of hearing Russell preach as a guest at her church many times. His students too. They'd been the blessed benefi- ciaries of a gifted communicator. And she, for the past ten years, had been the blessed recipient of his prayerful attentiveness and wisdom.

"A bit of quiet?" he asked.

"Please."

In the silence Kit centered herself in God's presence with her favorite breath prayer: *I can't. You can, Lord.* She couldn't watch over Wren to keep her safe or make her whole. God could. She couldn't ease Jamie's burden of worry. God could. She couldn't control or self-navigate the grief being tapped in her by Wren's struggles. But God could shepherd her through the valley of the shadow and enlarge her through the journey.

"I was talking with Wren's mom before you got here," she said after Russell offered an opening prayer, "and the whole time I was talking with her, I could see how the Lord was playing my own words to Jamie right back to me."

"God's good at that."

"Yes, he is." Holding up mirrors for prayerful reflection seemed to be a favorite move of his.

"What echoes were you hearing?" Russell asked.

Kit rubbed her brow slowly. "She was saying how tired she is, how helpless she feels, how she wonders if her prayers even make a difference. And then how feeling powerless feeds the cycle of wanting to take control, especially if it seems God isn't doing what she wants him to do." She paused. "And I said to her that being alongside a loved one who's suffering is exhausting."

Russell eyed her with compassion. "Is that how it feels for you right now? Exhausting?"

"Not because of Wren's needs, no. But because of what's getting stirred up in me while I'm alongside her, the grief points that get tapped as I think about my own losses."

Over the next half hour, she told Russell about the prayer collage exercise, the cup of guilt and regret she had been tempted to drink from again, and the letters she was writing and saving for Wren. "And of course, the way the Spirit works, the process of writing those is as much for me as it ever might be for her."

"What's that like for you?" Russell asked. "Writing them?"

She thought a moment, then said, "Hard. Painful. Freeing. Comforting. Another chance to see the larger picture of my healing journey and how Jesus has kept me company in it. So it's good." She shifted in her seat. "I had no idea when I invited Wren to stay with me that the Spirit would be working with me in such deep ways. I'm grateful for that. Always more for us to see and know and integrate. I just didn't realize there was so much that feels undone."

"Interesting word, that."

"Which?"

"*Undone.*"

"*Unfinished,* I should have said."

"But *undone* is intriguing."

Yes, it was. She smiled. "Nice catch."

"Do you want to stay with that or go somewhere else?"

She said, "I'll play with that one later. There's something else I'd like your ear on."

She told him, that morning, for the first time since Casey's death a month ago, Wren had asked to see his obituary. So Kit printed it out for her and sat beside her while she tried to read it. But looking at the obituary of a young man who should have had his life ahead of him had been yet another tap on her own heart. "I was too unwell to string any coherent and meaningful words together after Micah died, so Robert wrote his obituary. If he saved a copy, I don't know what happened to it. But I found it online this morning in an archive. Amazing, what you can find online." She removed from the coffee table a sheet of computer paper with a few sentences printed at the top. "I think I need to read it aloud to someone, and since you're here . . ."

Russell leaned forward in his seat, hands cupped in his lap in a posture of readiness to receive.

"Micah Jude Simpson, age seventeen," she began, "passed away in his sleep on March 31." That wasn't exactly true, she thought, but close enough. She'd found him in his bed, looking as if he had peacefully slipped away. A lump rose in her throat. "Micah is survived by his loving parents, Robert and Katherine Simpson . . ." *Survived by.* What a pair of words. She had barely survived his death, and their family hadn't survived intact. ". . . his sister, Sarah, and grandparents, Beverly and William Simpson and Constance and Edward Rhodes." All of them, except Sarah, now gone. "Micah was a senior at Kingsbury High School and planned to attend Central Michigan University to study veterinary medicine. He had a deep love for animals and books. A memorial service"— here her voice broke, and she took a moment to compose herself—

"will be held at First Church in Kingsbury on Saturday, April 3, at 1 p.m. Donations in Micah's honor may be made to the Kingsbury Animal Rescue Society."

She smoothed the paper on her lap, then carefully folded it into thirds. She would put it in an envelope when she returned home and tuck it in the box with the photos.

Looking up at Russell with tears blurring her vision, she said, "*Undone*. I guess that was the right word, wasn't it?"

He reached for a box of tissues on the end table and handed it to her.

"Thank you." She blew her nose. "So, here's what I'm thinking—that I might write obituaries for things that have died. I can't remember doing anything like that for my marriage. And I've certainly never done anything like that for the death of other dreams along the way."

"I love that idea, Katherine."

"Do you?"

"As long as you feel equipped and empowered to do it."

She reached for another tissue and wiped her eyes. "I don't think I came up with the idea on my own."

He smiled. "In that case . . ."

"Exactly." She threw the tissues into her wastebasket, then pressed the obituary to her chest. "'Let it be to me according to your word.'"

JANUARY 21

My dear Wren,

This week as a spiritual exercise, I've been writing obituaries. So far, I've written one for my marriage, one for my identity as wife, and one for my identity as Micah's mother. There's something healing about seeing the printed words on a page, marking the death of what was important and noting what was left behind in the wake of loss. There's also something fortifying about taking time to name what has survived: Katherine Simpson, who died on February 21, 1983, is survived by Katherine Rhodes. No, it's not the script I ever would have written for myself, but the story of that painful loss is a chapter in a larger story that continues to unfold. And by faith we trust that story has a happy ending.

I've been thinking about the Journey to the Cross Scriptures and the progression of my letters to you. Since my last one incorporated images of Gethsemane and Jesus drinking the cup for us, this one ought to be about Judas's betrayal. I go there reluctantly, aware of my own capacity to vilify the ones who have betrayed me, while distancing myself from my own likeness to Judas Iscariot.

We all know Judas's obituary. John gives it to us in his Gospel: Judas, son of Simon and one of the Twelve, betrayed him. The words "son of Simon" catch my attention. Judas was part of a family. His father must have been known in the early Christian community in order to be named. And what was it like for Simon, living with the shame and stigma of having been the father of such an infamous son? Though Judas's betrayal had cosmic consequences, I'm reminded through that simple phrase "son of Simon" that every betrayal has the power to affect families and communities, not just in the short term, but for generations to come. Not that I don't trust God's redemption of our sins. God is able to weave a glorious story using even our failures. But I'm sobered by the thought of the damage we cause and the violence we wreak on one another through our duplicity.

On paper, my marriage survived Micah by almost one year. But it was at Micah's funeral that I saw a woman I did not recognize greet Robert with a kiss on his cheek. In itself, that would not have been memorable or alarming. Many greeted me that day with a kiss of condolence. But her hand lingered on his longer than was fitting as she told him how sorry she was. Then she turned to me to express similar sympathy. Even though I was already plummeting into what would become debilitating depression, I was intuitive enough to see that she knew me in ways she should not have known me. And this could only have been through the intimacy of my husband's confiding in her. I felt betrayed.

It was after I returned home from the psychiatric hospital that I found a pair of unfamiliar shoes tucked into the dark recesses of my closet—the one personal item she had neglected to remove before my homecoming. Just when I thought I was coming up for air, I descended into the abyss again. Not unlike you, pushed under by the weight of grief and loss.

And yes, by a sense of betrayal. I hear it in your questions, wondering how Casey could have kept such significant secrets from you. Yours is a loss complicated by mystery—not only the mystery of his death, but the mystery of his life. What obituary do we write when we'll never know the truth about what was lost and why? Maybe what we write is an obituary for our need for closure and answers. Maybe someday you will write that one. Maybe there's one for me to write too.

I know how painful it was for you, not being able to go to Casey's funeral, and how wounding it was, being excluded and shunned by his family. Because of their anger and bitterness, you were denied an important opportunity to say goodbye to your friend in the presence of those who also love him and grieve his absence. I ache for you in this. But though we have no control over the narratives others weave about us, we don't need to be controlled by those narratives. Today I heard in you for the first time a determination to move forward in grieving Casey in a way that both honors him and brings comfort to you, regardless of what his family has done. I'm so glad you have decided to accept Hannah's invitation to lead a memorial service, and I will be honored to remember your beloved Casey with you.

In the meantime—in all these complex heartaches—we keep company with the One who did not withhold himself even from the pain of betrayal, who greeted Judas with the title "friend," even while knowing what he was about to do. And while Judas was the one who agreed to "hand him over," Jesus was the One who handed himself over first. What amazing love.

With you,

Kit

5

Awakened

JANUARY

On the last Saturday in January—six weeks after Casey's death—
Kit sat beside Hannah in the New Hope chapel, mentally replaying
the details from the memorial service that had just concluded.

Resurrection always startled and amazed.

As she listened to Wren laughing in the hallway with a few of
Casey's friends, she stared at the rooster painting Wren had completed in honor of him; the bright colors, thick layers of paint,
broad strokes, and swirl of movement in the feathers and head all
reminiscent of her beloved Vincent. Completing a painting would
have been a significant accomplishment under any normal circumstances. But summoning the strength and vision to paint it
while she was still struggling to undertake the simplest daily
tasks seemed miraculous. Who could have predicted that planning
a memorial service with her pastor would bring her to life?

"In all my years of conducting funerals and memorial services,"
Hannah said in a low, confidential tone, "I've never had that happen
before. Which is sad, I guess, when you think about it, that I can't

remember anyone ever coming to faith at one that I've led. I don't know. Maybe I haven't been bold enough in offering invitations. But I've never wanted to be manipulative or take advantage of people's grief." She paused. "Did I look as surprised as I felt?"

Kit smiled, remembering the expression of shock that had crossed Hannah's face when one of Casey's friends spoke up and said he thought it would be cool to follow Jesus. When another friend agreed, Hannah had led them both in prayer. "You handled it beautifully. It was a beautiful service. Such a gift to Wren. And to Casey's friends."

Hannah glanced toward the hallway, which was now empty. "I hope they'll move forward with faith. I invited them to come to church tomorrow, but I'm not sure Wayfarer is the best place for them. I can already see a few raised eyebrows if they come in smelling like pot."

It didn't take much effort for Kit to conjure memories of raised eyebrows toward Micah when he came to church wearing torn jeans and a grubby T-shirt or all black, sporting a new Mohawk. The eyebrows were for her too, a silent reproach that shouted, *Why don't you do something about him?* And she wanted to shout back, *Can't you understand how miraculous it is that he's even here?* But Micah wasn't blind, either, and there came a day when he decided that going to church wasn't worth his time.

How was it that Hannah, who had never met Casey, had been able to take Wren's stories about him and weave a narrative that captured his life with compassion, tenderness, and truth, while the man who had baptized Micah and led his confirmation class couldn't even call him by the correct name during the meeting to plan his funeral? And did anyone hear a word of hope or proclamation of the gospel at Micah's service? Kit couldn't remember anything their minister had said. Perhaps no word could have penetrated her grief.

She touched the stem of the flower Wren had placed on the chair where Casey had left his goodbye letter—a single sunflower she had plucked from the vases the florist had delivered. Were there flowers for Micah at his funeral? There must have been. Not ones she had ordered, though. Other people must have sent them. She hadn't known what to request for a seventeen-year-old boy. Robert must have taken care of the details. He must have taken care of most of the details in those weeks and months after Micah died. Had she ever thanked him for that? She couldn't remember. And it was too late now.

Hannah looked at her watch. "I've got to get going. Can I help you clean up in here?"

"No, no, you go ahead. I'm sure Wren will take care of it." If not today, then later. And if not on her own initiative, then with some gentle prompting. Now that she was showing signs of life again, it would be good for her to get back into a regular routine of cleaning. Kit rose with Hannah and gave her a hug. "Thank you for everything you've done for her."

"It's a privilege." Hannah tucked her Bible into her bag. "Let me know if there's anything else I can do."

"I will," Kit said, and walked with her down the hall.

"Were there flowers at the funeral?" Kit asked Sarah on the phone that night.

"What funeral?"

Kit picked up a dishrag and wiped off the kitchen counter. "Micah's."

"What do you mean?"

"Did we have flowers at Micah's funeral?" When Sarah didn't reply, Kit said, "I've been trying to remember today whether we had flowers at the church. We must have, right? People sent flowers?"

"Yes, I think so."

"I don't have any pictures from that day." She had searched through all her boxes of photos but hadn't found anything—not even a church bulletin. "Do you remember if anyone took any?"

"No idea. I've never seen any. Why?"

"Just wondering. There's so much I don't remember. I thought some photos might help."

It took a moment before Sarah said, "With what?"

Kit rinsed the cloth and draped it over the faucet. "Knowing that all the details I couldn't take care of were handled."

"Of course they were," Sarah said.

"Okay."

"I know there were flowers, Mom. I don't remember what kind. White ones, I think. Lilies, probably. Dad said no pink. I remember that."

Kit smiled. That sounded like something Robert would say. "You went with him to choose?"

"I must have."

"Thank you."

"For choosing flowers?"

She switched the phone to her other ear. "Not just for that. For all the ways I must have leaned on you back then."

"I didn't do much, Mom. I was away at school, remember?"

"I know."

"It was Dad who . . ."

"I know. He took care of all the practical things I couldn't do." She pictured Wren's rooster, its golden beak open, sounding the call to awaken. The Spirit was just as reliable and persistent a chanticleer.

Perhaps along with the obituaries she'd been writing, she could write Robert a letter to say she was sorry she hadn't expressed appreciation to him. Not just for the flowers. But for every burden he'd had to shoulder without her help. It seemed a significant oversight, not thinking about addressing that issue before now. Maybe she had. Maybe in her fog of grief and depression she had managed to thank him. It wouldn't hurt to do it again. And to be as specific in naming her gratitude as she had been in naming his sin.

JANUARY 27

My dear Wren,

It was a beautiful memorial service. I don't know which details you'll remember—maybe all the ones you wish to—but here's what will remain with me. I will remember Hannah speaking the words of our assurance and faith that death—no matter what kind of death—never has the final word. But death can feel like the most brutal exclamation point when we're consumed with grief. We wonder if the dawn will ever break again, if joy will ever return, if the promise that God will work all things together for the good of those who love him really is true. We need to be regularly reminded in community that the victory is won and that Christ really is risen from the dead. It's at times like these that our community of sorrow can become again a community of hope. And even joy.

I heard it in you today, and this I will remember and treasure too: the sound of your laughter ringing after Hannah offered a prayer to lead two of Casey's friends into life. In that moment the veil between here and eternity really was opened, and you joined in the joy of heaven singing over lost ones who had been found and brought home. By saying yes to honoring your friend with love and tenderness, you created a sacred space where others encountered Jesus. What a generous gift you gave.

You asked me the other day if Micah believed. I told you I wasn't sure what his thoughts about faith were at the end, but that I was confident in God's grace and the power of the cross. Today I was reminded of the promises spoken over Micah at his baptism. I was reminded that before our son knew his own name, God knew him and poured out his grace. I was reminded that there was a day when he claimed those promises for himself, even if he didn't fully understand what they meant. And though the darkness clouded his vision in the years that followed, I can trust the certainty of the promise that light shines in the darkness, and the darkness can never overcome it.

This is the confidence you painted in your rooster singing in the dark. It's a profound vision of hope. We spoke the other day about your worries that Casey was overcome with shame at the end and that his reference to a rooster crowing was one of despair. You worried he was more like

Judas, who lost hope, than Peter, who was able to press on. But I think his reference to the rooster reveals where his hope was rooted, even if he didn't fully understand it.

There's a detail in Luke's Gospel that isn't in the others, and it's always been a powerful one for me, that when the rooster crowed—at the very moment when Peter was saying for the third time that he didn't know Jesus—the Lord turned and looked at him. That's when Peter remembered: Jesus had predicted his failure. Not only had Peter claimed not to know Jesus, but up until that moment, he hadn't known himself. He hadn't yet seen within himself his own capacity for cowardice and duplicity. As painful as that moment must have been, it was also the moment when Peter's pride was broken. I hear in the rooster crow not only the sound of failure but also the sound of awakening. And both can be sounds of grace.

When Jesus predicted Peter's denial, he told him that Satan had demanded to sift the disciples like wheat, but he had prayed for Peter, that his faith would not fail and that once he turned back, he was to strengthen the others. It's interesting to me that Jesus did not pray for Peter not to fail. He did not pray for Peter to resist Satan and courageously defend him. No, Jesus prayed that Peter's faith would not fail after he failed, and that once he turned back, he would be like a stake in the ground, providing support for his brothers.

I like to think that's how he prays for me too. I like to think that's how he makes intercession for all of us, that when we fail—when, not if—he prays we will not lose courage but press forward in confidence of his mercy, love, and forgiveness. I like to think of his grace extending to those whose faith does fail, that he is tender to all who lose confidence in his love, to all for whom this world is just too hard.

I've stood on that precipice of despair. There were times after Micah died and after Robert left our marriage when I thought for sure my faith would fail. At times it did. That's when I had to borrow from the faith of others to keep persevering. There were times—many times—when I denied I knew Christ by turning aside to nurse my own anger, resentment, and self-pity. In those moments I hardly knew myself either. By God's grace I received the faith I needed in order to keep returning to him. But how can I fathom the mystery of my receiving faith when others do not? I'll write an obituary for my own unknowing in this too.

I marvel, though, at how another part of Jesus' prayer for Peter has also been answered in my life, and I know it has and will continue to be in yours as well: that when we have endured these dark nights of sorrow and testing, we will turn and strengthen others who are struggling to persevere. This is a gift we can offer others out of the deep chasms suffering has carved in us: the gift of compassion and comfort. When we see our own capacity for weakness and failure, we can be enlarged with patience and tenderness toward others. We can see and love with grace-washed eyes.

I wonder what was in Jesus' eyes when he looked at Peter? It couldn't have been surprise. He had predicted Peter's failure. It wasn't disappointment. He hadn't expected Peter to do any differently. I don't even think it was, "I told you so." I like to imagine that through his silent gaze, Jesus communicated a tender knowing that said, "I have prayed for you. Remember."

With you,

Kit

6

Accused

FEBRUARY

They weren't good enough, Wren said. She wasn't good enough. She would never be good enough to paint Jesus.

Kit sat down on a stool in Wren's studio at New Hope and stared at three different canvases she had erased with white paint. On one she could still perceive the faint outline of trees, which had probably been a riot of color and movement. *I wish you had let me see them first,* Kit wanted to say. But she didn't want to layer guilt or shame onto Wren's already fragile ego. Instead, she smiled and said, "Like your friend Vincent."

Wren stared at her, then nodded. She'd once told Kit that Vincent had ruthlessly destroyed his attempts to paint Jesus in Gethsemane. "But at least he was able to capture all the emotion of it through his trees. I can't even do that." She took off Casey's beanie, which she had recently washed, and swiped her brow with her paint-covered hand. "I'm sorry. But I think you'll have to use what you already have from the other artists. I'm not going to be able to do anything for the prayer stations."

"You've already done something. You've painted your beautiful rooster."

Wren shook her head. "It'll look ridiculous next to all the other professional ones."

"I'm not looking for professional. I'm looking for prayerful and evocative."

Wren gave an exasperated sigh.

There would be no arguing with her about it. Either she would be led through her resistance and fear, or she would give in to the accusatory voices in her own head. "C'mon," Kit said, rising from the stool. "Walk away from it for a while. I always find that helps when I'm feeling stuck." She motioned toward the Van Gogh books on the table. "Besides. I've got another project I need your help with—choosing art for the walls, remember? I want to re-envision the whole space here, and I need your input. Let's take a walk together."

For the next half hour, they strolled through hallways and lounge spaces, discussing which prints would be best suited for each area. Wren had many ideas from Vincent's work, including one of a sower Kit hadn't seen before. "I love everything about that," she said as Wren held the book open against the wall. "The movement. The colors. Even the tree, the way it's leaning, with branches cut off. All of it speaks to hope."

Wren nodded and traced her finger around the bright golden sun. "See? It's like a halo behind the sower's head."

Kit laughed. "You're right! I'm not sure I would have seen that without help. But that's a profound statement, isn't it? Like a hallowing of the work of sowing seeds." She stepped back to picture it on the wall. "I can't think of any better statement to make about the work we long to do here. Sow seeds and trust God with the growth." Casting the seeds was simple enough. It was the incubation and waiting time that was hard.

"There's one I haven't destroyed."

Kit was startled out of her own thoughts. "What's that?"

"A painting," Wren said. "There's one I haven't erased. But it's not very good either."

Kit smiled at her. "Sometimes we need others to help us discern the truth about such things. May I see it?"

"It's not done. And I already know it won't be good enough for the prayer journey."

"But maybe there's a seed of something true in it," Kit said, and followed her back to the studio.

Clearly inspired by Vincent's olive groves, Wren's trees appeared almost human, writhing and twisting. Streaks of red stained the ground, testifying to a struggle in the darkness. This was no serene garden. This was the place of pressing. Of crushing. And there was no escape.

Kit gripped the edge of the canvas with both hands. *Unless a grain of wheat falls into the ground and dies . . .*

"I told you it wasn't very good," Wren said, reaching to take it from her.

"Wren." Kit gently motioned for her to step back so she could keep studying it. "You've captured something here. I just need a minute with it."

Kit let her gaze drift slowly across the canvas, taking in the thick brushstrokes and splotches of color for the leaves, noting the stark outlines of the trunks and one prominent root reaching in vain for a place to cling. But it was the middle of the painting that kept drawing her attention—the empty space between the trees, framed by the menacing, arching branches. She pointed to it. "Did you deliberately paint this in the center?"

"The gap, you mean?" Wren asked. "It's just between the trees."

"I know. But it looks like it has a specific shape, even three-dimensional. Like a stone. Or a seed."

Wren leaned forward for a closer look, then shook her head slowly. "No, I didn't put it there. Not consciously, anyway." She traced her finger around it. "But I see what you mean. It looks like a cave right in the center, doesn't it? A hole."

"Or a tomb," Kit said.

Wren stared at her, eyes wide. "A tomb," she murmured.

That void between the trees—like a stone that crushed, a seed that died, a cave that concealed, a tomb that held—that was the way out. The only way out of the place of pressing was by entering the darkness and submitting to death. And trusting that the void was not a hopeless chasm but a fertile space, a womb for resurrection life.

Unless a grain of wheat falls to the ground and dies, Kit thought, *it remains alone. But if it dies, it bears much fruit.*

She touched the center of the painting. "Don't destroy this one, Wren. Please."

FEBRUARY 6

My dear Wren,

I've watched you agonize this week in your studio, fighting the voices of accusation in your own head and second-guessing your gifts. When I first asked you months ago to prayerfully consider painting the stations for me, I told you I wouldn't hover or interfere with your process, but that I would take on a measure of responsibility for your wellness while you painted. I told you I didn't want it to become a burden or source of anxiety for you, but that I hoped you would discover something new and life-giving about Jesus' presence and love while you paint and pray.

Though I've seen you discouraged and heard the frustration and weariness in your voice, I sense this is a battle for you to fight and win— the battle of silencing the voice of the accuser and listening instead to the voice of the One who has named you his own and who has prepared in advance good works for you to do.

You're doing those good works, whether it feels like it or not. You're saying yes to being stretched and formed, not only as you paint but as you continue to fight to be well. I'm proud of you. I'm proud of you every time you say yes to getting out of bed in the morning to face the burdens and challenges of the day. I'm proud of you for persevering and continuing to choose life. I understand the battle, not just as a distant memory or experience in my past, but as an ongoing struggle. We choose and keep on choosing. Every day.

But the voice of the accuser is a siren song, and every time we listen to it and agree with what it says, we consent to waging violence—not only against ourselves but against others.

I remember after Robert left and married Carol, I was so consumed with bitterness and self-pity, I could hardly breathe. Over and over again I rehearsed the injury of what they had done and everything they had taken from me through their sin. (I hadn't intended to write about this when I began this letter, but since I've begun, I'll finish.) One day I was naming again to God their sin—not in the productive and fruitful mode of letting it go in order to forgive, but in the stuck-record mode of nursing my wounds. That's when I heard the Spirit address me with a penetrating word that was both convicting and liberating: "They already have an accuser. Do not join him in his work."

I was silenced. That day I made a decision: I would seek to speak the truth about sin without layering condemnation on top of it—not for myself, or for others. I'd love to say that's been my consistent habit these many years since, but I haven't always succeeded at it. Through practice, though, I've become quicker to recognize the voice of the accuser and resist it.

Here's the tricky thing. Sometimes what the accuser speaks is true, especially regarding our sin. But the accusation is meant to destroy us with shame and guilt. In those moments I use the accuser's voice as a prompt to remind me I have a Savior who has paid the price for all my sin. I use the accuser's voice as a prod to drive me to Jesus to receive his grace and mercy. "Thank you so much for reminding me how desperately I need Jesus," I'll say when I hear the voice. "I'll talk with him right now." Funnily enough, I find the voice is silenced. Especially when the only thing it's accomplishing is to drive me to the cross.

I haven't gone in the direction I intended when I began writing this letter. But rather than crossing through it or destroying it completely, I'll trust that something here might be helpful to you. Like your painting was for me.

Here's what I planned to say. I planned to write about Jesus facing Pilate and the Jewish leaders and keeping silent before every false accusation levied against him. He is a marvel to me. Every time Robert accused me of being "crazy" or "impossible to live with," every time he blamed me for the breakdown of our marriage—and yes, I contributed to it, no question—I lashed out in anger, seeking to defend myself and wound him in return. That got me nowhere. And my anger and vindictiveness only confirmed the worst of what he said about me.

I hear you rehearse the accusations made against you—not only the ones you voice about your lack of skill as an artist, but the ones you've internalized about Casey and his death. Others have borne false witness against you. And you have borne it against yourself. May the One who himself endured false witness strengthen you and deliver you from this.

Jesus was able to keep silence in the face of his accusers because he knew they didn't speak the truth, and he didn't need to defend himself. More than that, he knew who and whose he was. That's what I'm praying for you as you press forward, that you will resist the work of the accuser, in all its alluring forms, and stand firm in the identity God has given you in Christ, that you are his beloved child, and nothing seen or unseen—nothing in your past, present, or future—has the power to separate you from his great and steadfast love.

With you,

Kit

7

Bearing the Cross

ASH WEDNESDAY

She had planned to go to her own church for the Ash Wednesday worship service. But when Wren took the initiative and invited Kit to join her at Wayfarer for an evening service, she gratefully accepted. Any move toward participating in community life needed to be affirmed.

In a darkened sanctuary that smelled faintly of candle wax, Hannah invited the congregation into a season of reflection, self-examination, and repentance—a season to take seriously the call to journey with Jesus to the cross. "We're called to remember Jesus' own words, 'Whoever wants to be my disciple must deny themselves, take up their cross, and follow me.'" And that, Hannah said, was a far more radical call than giving up chocolate or caffeine for forty days. "It's a call to die to ourselves so we can live more fully in Christ. And that dying can take on many different forms."

The living, too, Kit thought as she watched shadows flicker on the walls.

At the designated time, they went forward to receive the mark of the ashes as a symbol of embracing Christ's call. From her place beside Wren, Kit watched Hannah gently brush aside Wren's hair from her forehead, the dark strands no longer oily and flat—a silent testimony to her emerging hope and renewal.

With her thumb covered in black ash, Hannah made a downward stroke. "Wren, count yourself dead to sin"—she dipped her thumb into the bowl of ashes again before making the horizontal cross—"and alive in Christ." Her hand still resting on Wren's forehead, she whispered, "The Lord bless you and keep you."

Kit brushed her own hair back and leaned forward to receive. "Katherine." Hannah dipped her thumb into the bowl, ashes sprinkling onto the ground. "Count yourself dead to sin"—the tip of her nail scratched the vertical line—"and alive in Christ." It wasn't merely a horizontal stroke. Hannah's thumb moved across and upward, as if marking the victory even there. "The Lord make his face to shine upon you and give you peace," Hannah said.

Wren turned, her gaze landing on Kit's forehead as if searching for a mirror to reflect the image marked on her own. As they returned to their seats, Kit glanced around the sanctuary at people bearing the cross, saints and sinners, all of them, each unique in their struggles and joys, yet united by a common need, longing, and hope. Together in the journey to death. And to life.

Wren fell asleep before changing her clothes or washing her face. Kit, who had for the past several months been in the habit of checking on her before heading to bed herself, covered her with an afghan. She woke briefly, mumbled her thanks, and went back to sleep.

Kit was about to turn off the nightstand lamp when the sight of Wren's head on her pillow and the cross on her skin brought to mind a detail she'd forgotten. Steadying herself against the desk, she inhaled slowly, matching her breath with prayer.

In her years as a chaplain she had marked those lines on many foreheads of the sick and dying. She had marked the cross to remind them they belonged to Christ, in life and in death. She had marked the cross to declare their trust and hope.

She looked again at Wren, her body still, the blanket beneath her chin.

Micah had lain in much the same way the morning she found him, his body still, his blanket pulled to his chin. She had tried to rouse him. She had tried in vain to find his breath. But there was no life.

And why did she do what she did next? Was it habit or hope when she brushed aside the hair from his forehead and made the sign of the cross on his cold skin? What did she hope the Lord would do? Raise him from the dead? Or reassure her that in life and in death, her son belonged to him?

FEBRUARY 15

My dear Wren,

You came down to breakfast this morning, the cross still visible on your forehead. It was that cross that spoke to me last night, reminding me of something I hadn't thought about in years. Painful as it was, remembering, it was another opportunity for me to receive Jesus' comfort and love.

I was the one who found Micah after he died. I remember how peaceful he looked, as if he had only just fallen asleep. In my work, first as a hospice chaplain and later as a chaplain at St. Luke's, I saw many hard, labored, and "ugly" deaths. Micah's was not that. Robert wrote in his obituary that he died in his sleep. It wasn't the whole truth—Robert probably wanted to do what he could to protect Micah and our family from widespread gossip and shame—but it was true that he died while he was asleep. I'm grateful he did not suffer terror and trauma in dying. A small consolation in the midst of the horror.

I don't remember much about that morning. At some point, I must have shouted for Robert to come. I don't remember Micah being carried from the house. I don't remember who gathered to mourn with us that day. But I remember leaning forward to touch my son's cheek as he lay in his bed. I remember brushing the hair from his forehead as I had done many times. And last night I remembered how I marked on his forehead the sign of the cross. I am grateful for the reminder.

The excavation of a single memory often brings others to the surface. As I think of Hannah's words about the call to take up our own cross and follow Christ, I remember the ones who helped me bear the cross of sorrow and suffering by bearing the cross of self-sacrifice and love. I've told you about the chaplain who cared for me in the psychiatric hospital, how he companioned me from death to life. Today I remember colleagues who laid down their lives for me by giving me their vacation days so I could not only take the time I needed in the hospital, but also take the time I needed to recover afterward. Such an extraordinary gift of love.

Even then—even after I had gratefully received their gifts and taken months to rest—it was clear I could not return to my hospice work. I could not minister to the dying in their homes. It was not safe for me. I could not minister in an ongoing way to their families. It wasn't safe for me, and it wasn't good pastoral care for them. It was a couple of years before I was well enough to return to chaplaincy work. And even then, I had to be continually mindful of the triggers that could spiral me into depression again. But I had the gift of skilled and compassionate colleagues alongside to hold me accountable and pray for my wholeness as I said yes to the call I believed God had given me. They bore the cross with me.

I think of Simon of Cyrene, forced by a Roman soldier to bear Christ's cross. I wonder if part of him resisted, even while having to obey. I wonder if he understood the gift he was giving Jesus by removing the physical burden from his bruised and bloodied back. I wonder if he understood afterward what an honor and privilege had been given to him, to literally carry the cross of Christ. For Christ.

Bearing the cross is an honor and privilege, as costly as it is. I'm glad Hannah reminded us about that as we prepared to receive the symbol of our faith and our call.

I think, too, of the words my pastor speaks when he places the ashes on our foreheads: "Remember that you are dust. And to dust you shall return."

One year a friend complained to me that the words were morbid and depressing. I guess they could be. But to me they are a necessary counterbalance in our life of discipleship. We are human. We are finite. We are limited. We are dust. Beloved dust that will be given resurrection bodies, yes. But still, dust. Those words are a reminder of our mortality. This life is temporary. And because it is short and fleeting, that makes the call to take up the cross and follow Jesus even more urgent. But we follow in our weakness and our frailty, in our stumbling and our failures. We follow in grace and by the power of the Spirit.

For my Micah and your Casey, the end of temporary came far too soon. But by faith in God's goodness and mercy, we trust they were marked with a cross that will not fade or wash away. And perhaps I will continue to mark the sign on my forehead. And remember.

With you,

Kit

8

Lament

FEBRUARY

At the sound of her cell phone buzzing on her desk, Kit glanced up from her retreat notes. It was unusual for Jamie to call while she was at New Hope. Normally, she called before or after work.

"Did I get you at a bad time?" Jamie asked.

"No, just reviewing some notes for the retreat tomorrow. How are you?"

"I just got a call from Wren. She doesn't sound good."

Kit stiffened, mentally scanning the last few hours: a breakfast together at the house and extended time in her studio. She'd asked Wren to re-clean one of the women's bathrooms, but she hadn't seemed upset or offended by that. Just apologetic. *Distracted by painting,* she'd said. And Kit had said, *No worries.* But maybe she had managed to disguise a deeper sense of shame. "I saw her about half an hour ago. She seemed okay."

Jamie said, "She just got a text from Casey's mother, who found out about the memorial service and wasn't at all happy about it."

Kit exhaled slowly. "Oh, no. I'll go talk to her."

"I'm sorry to bother you, Kit, it's just . . ."

"I know." Any little trigger could send her into a dangerous place. "How about if I ask her to check in with you later? That way we don't—"

"I know," Jamie said. "I know I promised not to talk about her behind her back. But I'm worried about this one."

Kit promised to call if there was an emergency, then opened her office door and headed down the hallway. Wren's studio was closed. Kit knocked. No answer. She pushed the door open a few inches. Not there.

A few minutes later she found her in the chapel, near the painting of Jesus on the cross, seated in the chair Wren had marked with a tiny strip of masking tape to memorialize the place where Kit had found Casey's goodbye letter. "Your mom called me."

Wren nodded. "Your office door was closed."

Kit sat down beside her. "You can always check with Gayle to see if I'm meeting with someone. But if it's just me working in there, I don't mind you interrupting."

"Okay."

Kit motioned toward the phone on Wren's lap. "Casey's mom contacted you?"

"Yeah." She shifted in her chair. "Turns out, one of the guys who said he thought it would be cool to follow Jesus—well, his mom knows Casey's mom and mentioned to her what a miracle it was, him coming to faith at Casey's service."

Oh, West Michigan. It was such a small world.

"So basically," Wren said, "this amazing thing—because it *was* amazing, like Casey had something to do with leading him there, you know?—turns into this awful, ugly, hateful thing." She bit her lip and touched her screen. "Here. You can read it."

Kit took the phone. Wren hadn't exaggerated. The words spit venom from the screen. *How dare she?* Her actions were "unforgiveable" and "selfish," a "wound and insult to his family," and especially to his wife, who was, his mother said, *his wife*, much as Wren might have wished otherwise, much as she had tried to undermine and destroy that reality by refusing to let go of her relationship with him, even after he married. "What's done is done," his mother concluded, but Wren would have to live with the consequences of the irreparable harm she had caused, and she hoped she would feel the full weight of it.

"Dear God," Kit murmured as she turned the phone upside-down and set it aside. "Can you delete it?"

"If I want to."

"I hope you will."

She shrugged. "That's not all."

Kit waited.

"I've been following his wife online so I could get updates and see all the baby photos. Like I could keep watch and pray, because I think Casey would want that, even with all the secrets he kept from me. And I guess I was also hoping that someday Brooke might post something that would give more information about what happened, what he intended." She reached for her phone and started scrolling. "Maybe she figured out that I was tracking her—maybe his mother warned her or something—because when I tried to check her page a little while ago, her profile had been made private." Wren's voice broke. "So, that's the end. I'm completely cut off from him now." Her shoulders heaved. Kit wrapped her arm around her and held her while she cried.

That night, after she and Wren finished their evening prayers together, Kit reached into her notebook on the kitchen table and removed seven dated envelopes from the pockets. "I was going to save these for another time, but maybe it's more important not to try to control when you read them, or how you read them."

Wren eyed her quizzically.

"I've been writing you letters. A bit like what you suggested, with my own story wrapped around some of the prayer station Scriptures. But rather than putting something out publicly, I decided to write it just for you."

Wren took the stack from her. "Thank you. That means a lot to me."

"Whatever's helpful, receive it with my love. Whatever's not helpful, disregard. But given what you received today from Casey's mother, maybe something in here will speak to you and give you comfort."

Wren reached for her hand. "Companions in sorrow," she said. And Kit nodded.

Companions in sorrow. Kit gazed out at the group gathered for the second session of the Lenten retreat Saturday morning. Wren had asked if she could attend, even if she had missed the first one. Kit had hardly been able to conceal her surprise and delight when she replied, "Of course." She would be teaching on lament, she told her, and Wren had said, "Good."

And so, after offering an opening prayer, Kit began with a story she often told when she taught about lament, how years ago a friend had sent her a link to a television talk show featuring a guest who had been born without arms or legs. Before showing the audience the introductory video, however, the host gave this admonishment: "Anyone with a complaint on the tip of your tongue, shut your mouth. This video is going to shut your mouth." And then the audience watched the inspiring footage of someone conquering a profound disability.

"That's the voice many of us internalize," Kit said, "the voice that tells us our suffering is nothing compared to what others suffer and that we have no right to complain. No right to grieve." Much of her time, first as a chaplain and then as a spiritual director, she said, was spent giving permission to those who had swallowed their pain to spit it out. "Because if we aren't offering our pain to God, we have an enemy who would love to turn it toxic and use it for his own purposes."

With her scribbled outline on the podium in front of her, Kit talked about lament being a spiritual discipline for the brave, how

the lament psalms were raw, bold, and even accusatory, pleading—
sometimes demanding—that God act in a manner consistent
with his revealed character. "These are the protest psalms," Kit
said, "the psalms that cry out for the kingdom to come, the
prayers that help us return to the love of God when we doubt the
love of God. These are the prayers of the bewildered, the broken,
and the hopeful. These aren't the prayers of atheists. Atheists
expect nothing from God, so they're never disappointed by God.
But if we have experienced the mercy and love and power of a
good and generous God—if we have seen God intervene in
amazing ways in our lives or in the lives of others—then we're
bound to be left feeling confused and disappointed when God
seems silent and distant, when God seems deaf to our groaning
or unconcerned about our needs and our pain. The question is,
Will we offer that disappointment and sense of betrayal to God?
Will we lament in God's direction, or will we walk away?"

Kit's gaze fell on Wren, who was looking intently at her with
the same probing expression that had accompanied her question
months ago: Do you share your story at the retreats you lead?

How long did that moment of discernment last, when Kit kept
silent before the group, listening for the Spirit to say yes or no?
Long enough for a few in the group to begin shifting in their seats.
Someone coughed. She glanced down at her notes, then stepped
away from the podium.

"When I was almost forty," she said, "I lost my beloved son
to a drug overdose. In my grief, I lost my hope in a good and
loving God. I could have lost my life, I was that despairing. At

the psychiatric hospital where I went to try to recover, a chaplain read lament psalms to me when I could not read or pray myself. He gently pointed me to the cross. And he encouraged me to listen deeply to the voice of Jesus crying out, My God, my God, why have you forsaken me?"

At her table toward the back of the room, Wren pressed her hand to her heart. And nodded.

FEBRUARY 24

My dear Wren,

It blessed me so deeply tonight when you asked if I would be willing to continue writing letters to you. I'm honored to hear that my words have been a help and a comfort to you. It's been a rich journey for me, reflecting on how the Lord has met and shaped me through suffering. We forget so much over the years. And we can become immune to the power of our own stories.

I don't think you'll ever know the significance of you nudging me to share mine, first with you and then today, on a larger scale, with others. I had been so worried about calling attention to myself that I neglected the opportunity to call attention to Christ in very specific ways. And though I've often marveled at how the Spirit has moved during the retreats at New Hope, today I was aware of what was opened in others because of what the Lord opened in me.

Thank you. Thank you for reminding me that though our laments are intensely personal, they are meant to be offered in community. I've taught this to others. I've neglected it for myself.

I'm reminded of the women weeping as they followed Jesus to the cross. What a gift that they had one another to share the burden of their sorrow.

Though Jesus tells them not to weep for him, he calls them to weep for themselves and their children. Not only will they bear the agony of watching their beloved friend and rabbi die, but some of them will live to see the brutal destruction of Jerusalem. And for some of them, the pain, he says, will be too much to bear. "They will say to the mountains, Fall on us! And to the hills, Cover us!"

That's what it feels like when we're in the depths of despair, doesn't it? We want it to be over. We may not be tempted to bring about the end by our own hand, but we long for mountains to fall on us so we'll be free from the anguish. You and I have lived that. Thank God, we lived through it. Sometimes, we live with it. Always, we live in spite of it. What a gift to live it together.

With you,

Kit

9

Stripped

FEBRUARY

"How about a field trip today?" Kit asked as they finished putting away the breakfast dishes.

Wren said, "I've got some cleaning to do, after the retreat and everything."

"That can wait. No one will be there today, and I need an extra day off." There would come a day, Kit thought, when she would need more than a bit of extra time to recover. And perhaps that day was coming sooner than she expected, much as she loved her work. She leaned back to stretch.

"What did you have in mind?" Wren asked.

"I thought we could go and do a prayer walk. My church has its own version of the stations of the cross in the sanctuary."

Wren hesitated. "I'm not sure. I'm worried I might be intimidated by them, like they'll be one more reminder of why I shouldn't be trying to paint them myself."

Kit had already thought of that. "They're wood carvings, completely different than what you're doing."

Wren appeared to be mulling this over. "Okay," she said after a while. "That might be okay."

Before she could change her mind, Kit retrieved her bag and shepherded her out the door.

Kingsbury's Church of the Redeemer, where she had worshiped ever since her divorce, incorporated eight Scripture texts, beginning not in the Garden of Gethsemane, but with Jesus before Pilate. After alerting the church administrator that they would be in the sanctuary, Kit joined Wren in front of that carving.

"It's like you wrote in your letter," Wren murmured, "about Jesus being in front of his accusers and not needing to defend himself. There's such strength in him. Like Pilate is the one who can't bear to make eye contact."

Kit said, "I love that you see that. *Strength* is the perfect word." She lightly touched Wren's shoulder. "Take your time going through them. There's one particular one I want to meditate on, so I'm going to start there."

Leaving her to ponder and pray, Kit walked to the fifth prayer station at the front right corner of the sanctuary and sat down. *Jesus Is Stripped of His Garments*, read the sign on the wall. She let her gaze wander across the carving, noting the posture of the soldiers as they reached to grab what Jesus was already handing over without resistance: his outer garment. Soon he would be humiliated by having even his tunic stripped away. And while he hung on a cross, naked, the soldiers would cast lots for it, esteeming its value far more highly than they esteemed a man's life.

The longer she studied the scene, the more her anger escalated, a pointed contrast to the peaceful determination on Jesus' face. He was a marvel.

Stripped. Shamed. Mocked. Exposed. Humiliated. All of this he endured without once lashing out in anger or resentment.

How differently she had responded when she was stripped and exposed, publicly maligned not only by the one who had given her his vow of fidelity, but by the woman who had wrested from her the life she had known for more than twenty years as Robert's wife.

Truly, Jesus was a marvel. The restraint of the Son of God as he submitted himself to the cross never ceased to astonish and humble her.

She glanced over her shoulder to mark Wren's progress, only to find her kneeling in front of the carving of Jesus before Pilate, head in her hands.

"I kept thinking of what you wrote about the accuser," Wren said as they drove home. "I've been wanting to write back to his mother, to explain myself and tell her why I wanted to honor Casey. He wasn't only her son and Brooke's husband and Estelle's dad. He was my friend. And I'll always love him."

"Of course you will."

Wren stared out the car window. "He was like a brother to me. I love my brother and sisters, but it's not the same having siblings who are so much younger. They have each other. I had Casey." Her voice broke. "She acts like there was something inappropriate between us. There never was. Ever. We never dated, never even wanted to. Brooke claims we were emotionally codependent, and I'll give her that. I will. There was a lot that was unhealthy about the ways I tried to rescue him and how I relied on him for support. And I guess part of me wants to be able to say that to Brooke, to tell her I'm sorry for trying to lean on Casey, even after they got married. But how do I do that now? How do I try to ask for forgiveness when they want nothing to do with me?"

"Or when asking for it might not be safe or wise for you right now," Kit said quietly.

Wren turned to look at her. "Right. I guess that's right. But Jesus talked a lot about forgiveness and needing to move toward someone if they have something against you. And Brooke and his mom have lots against me, even if a lot of it isn't true." She sat back in her seat, hands clutched in her lap. "I feel like they've blocked me from doing what might help me move forward. And I don't know what to do with that."

Eyes fixed on the road, Kit took a moment to decide how much input to offer. "I love your desire to ask for forgiveness and your willingness to own what you see as your responsibility, Wren. I'm sure Dawn and Hannah can give you wise and prayerful counsel about what's best for you to do right now. But as far as someone having the power to keep you from moving forward in healing if you can't move toward them in reconciliation, that's not true. No one has the power to hold you hostage to guilt or shame or regret. We hold our own keys to that prison, and the cell door locks from the inside." She glanced briefly toward Wren. "So, whatever process of forgiveness you need to work through, you can begin by having a conversation with God about receiving his forgiveness and forgiving yourself, even if the others never forgive you. And you can begin a process of forgiving them for the wounds they've inflicted on you."

Wren sighed slowly. "I used to talk to the women at Bethel House about the difference between forgiveness, reconciliation, and trust. Guess I need to pay attention to my own words, don't I?"

Kit smiled. "Don't we all?"

FEBRUARY 28

My dear Wren,

I've been thinking this week about the word "stripped." I've been pondering all that Jesus allowed others to strip away from him—not only his physical clothing, but also his reputation and dignity.

There was a time in my life when my dignity and reputation were stripped from me too. But oh, how I resisted that particular death. It was hard enough, being so utterly stripped of my emotional and mental strength that I needed to seek help at a psychiatric hospital. I remember crying when the staff confiscated from me my cross necklace and a silver bracelet my parents gave me on my sixteenth birthday. Though I received all my personal items back when I was discharged, there was something humiliating about being deemed such a danger to myself that I couldn't be trusted to wear the jewelry that gave me courage and consolation. I was allowed to keep my wedding band, I remember. And that, in retrospect, was an irony.

It was while I was at the hospital that stories about my breakdown were whispered and shared under the guise of prayer requests: "Pray for Kit. Did you hear what happened???" Gossip, in any form, is violence. By the time I returned home, people had constructed their own narratives about responsibility and blame. This helped pave the way for Robert's exit, which, by many, was viewed as understandable, given my "instability."

For a long time I tried desperately to justify and defend myself, to restore my reputation by manipulating others' opinions of me. It's exhausting, futile work. St. Francis of Assisi wisely said that who we are before God is who we are. No more, no less. We are naked. Seen. Stripped. Exposed. Loved.

It's a comfort to me that Jesus allowed himself to be stripped. And so he accompanies us in all of our undefended—and yes, terrifying—vulnerabilities and shameful exposures. He is our covering. And he is our defender.

I've never forgotten a dream I had during that season of my life. I dreamed that Robert and Carol and a group of others were throwing bricks at my head. I kept trying to duck and defend myself, but it was no use. Suddenly, Jesus stepped in front of me. He shielded me from them, taking the blows himself. Then he stooped and began picking up the bricks. I wasn't sure at first what he was going to do with them. But as I watched, he laid them on the ground, making a path. Then he took my hand, and we walked together along that path, through the crowd.

As I prayed with the images from that dream, I saw with fresh eyes not only how Jesus accompanies us through such trials, but also how he paves for us the difficult path to healing and freedom when he prays, "Father, forgive them. They don't know what they're doing." It's hard enough to forgive others when they actually recognize and confess their sin and ask for forgiveness. But when they go blithely on their way, unaware of—or unconcerned about—the destruction they've caused? That's another kind of stripping, the stripping away of my desire to make someone see the truth. And repent. In other words, it's a stripping away of my desire for control. And that stripping, I know, is one my flesh will always resist. No matter how old I grow.

With you,

Kit

10

Pierced

MARCH

"You look tired, Mom."

Kit laughed. Her daughter had never had any trouble being direct. "Nice to see you too!"

Sarah stamped the snow from her boots on the front porch, then leaned in to kiss Kit on the cheek. "I'm just saying, I see it in your eyes."

"In that case, then, looks aren't deceiving. I *am* tired." She peered over Sarah's shoulder at her white Subaru in the driveway. "The girls aren't with you?"

"No, Morgan said to say hi, but she's working on a term paper and didn't feel like she could take a break. And Jess says she's sorry, but she's studying for AP exams."

Ah, well. Maybe next time. "Understood," she said. "'Hi' back to them."

Sarah hung her coat and scarf in the closet. "Is Wren here?"

"No, she's having coffee with a friend."

"Oh, that's good. So she's . . . ?"

"Yes. Doing okay."

Sarah nodded. She knew better than to ask any more probing questions than that. "I'm sorry I haven't had a chance to come see you, Mom. January and February passed in a total blur."

"No, it's fine. I haven't had much margin for visits."

"Yeah. About that." Sarah followed her to the kitchen. "I'm worried about the toll this is taking on you, having her here." It wasn't the first time Sarah had voiced her concern.

"I like having the company."

"I know. You've said that. But this is more than 'company.' It's not just having someone in your house, it's the responsibility and burden that comes with keeping watch over her. And that's exhausting."

Kit wasn't going to argue that point. "She's doing better, though. I think she's turned a corner again."

Sarah leaned against the sink. "Morgan still talks about you not being able to spend Christmas with us."

"I know. I'm sorry. There was no way to leave her then, and she wasn't up to coming with me." Kit retrieved the teakettle and motioned for Sarah to step aside from the sink.

Sarah shifted out of the way. "You know how these things go, Mom, how it can improve for a while and then . . ."

"I know."

"So, what's the end game here? I mean, how long have you committed to letting her stay?"

Kit turned on the faucet and let cold water splash onto her

hand before filling the kettle. "No end date," she said, "just a prayerful holding of it all."

Sarah sighed slowly.

"Oh, don't sigh at me. Being prayerful isn't an excuse."

"I know. That's not what the sigh was for."

"What, then?" She set the kettle on its base and flipped on the switch.

"I heard about the retreat."

Kit stiffened, her back still turned toward her daughter. "What do you mean?"

"The one you did last week? Someone who was there was telling a friend about it, and that friend emailed me."

The West Michigan fishbowl. Again. She glanced over her shoulder. "And?"

"She told me you talked about Micah and being at the psychiatric hospital. Did you tell the group you were suicidal?"

"Suicidal? Heavens no. Where on earth would someone have gotten that idea?"

"What exactly did you say, then?"

She wasn't going to have this conversation standing in the middle of her kitchen floor. She gestured toward the table. "Here, have a seat." When she removed two mugs from the cupboard, she noticed her hand was shaking.

What had she said? She scanned her memory as she sat down across from Sarah. "We were talking about lament, about the need to offer our pain to God in prayer. And I decided—at what I sensed was a prompt from the Spirit—to share a bit of my own journey with grief and how the lament psalms helped save my life. Or rather, how God used them to rescue me from despair and move me toward hope."

"So, you did say you were suicidal."

"I didn't say I was suicidal now. But back then, yes. That's why I went to the hospital in the first place, because I didn't trust what I might do."

Sarah shook her head slowly. "That's not what some people heard."

Kit sat up straighter in her chair. "I don't have control over what people hear."

"But you have control over what you say, Mom. And how you say it. And I don't understand why—after all these years—why you've decided to share the story publicly now."

"Because it's my story."

"It's not just yours, Mom."

"I'm his mother. I can tell that story."

"And I was his sister. And the daughter whose mom had a nervous breakdown and whose parents split up because her dad had an affair. Did you tell that story too?"

"Of course not. I didn't mention you."

"No, I mean about Dad. Did you talk about him too?"

Kit bristled. She hadn't. But didn't she have the freedom to tell that part of her story? If she wanted? Couldn't she be trusted to tell that story in a way that didn't cast blame but spoke the truth and pointed to Jesus? "I didn't mention your father. Only Micah. And my own journey with grief." She wouldn't mention the letters or conversations with Wren. Sarah didn't need to know she'd named her grief over Robert in a different context.

"I just wish we could have talked about it first, Mom. I wish you had told me you were thinking about sharing your story in that kind of context."

"And what if I had? What would you have said?"

Sarah rubbed her forehead slowly.

"If I had thought to ask your permission first, what would you have said?"

"You didn't need my permission. That's not what I meant."

"That's what it sounded like." Kit leaned her elbows on the table.

"I'm just saying, Mom, I would have appreciated the conversation. You know how small a community this is. Sharing those details doesn't just impact you, it impacts me too."

Okay. That was fair. "I'm sorry," Kit said. "You're right. Please forgive me."

Sarah reached across the table to grasp her hand. "I'm worried, that's all. It seems like Wren is tapping all kinds of triggers for you because of what happened with Micah."

"I'm being mindful of that."

"I hope so."

"I am. And regardless of what someone thought they heard me say on Saturday, I stand by my decision to say it. If it helped one person in the room . . . if my story about grief and despair and shame helps one single person, it's worth it to me."

The front door creaked open. "Kit?"

She squeezed Sarah's hand, then let go. "In here, Wren."

"I saw the car in the driveway and . . ." She came around the corner, still wearing her coat and boots. "Oh, hey, Sarah."

Sarah gave a slight wave. "Hey, Wren."

"Sorry to interrupt."

Kit rose to make their tea. "It's okay. Would you like to have tea with us?"

"No, thanks. Mara's waiting for me in the car. I wanted to show her the paintings I'm working on but don't have a key to the building. Is it okay if we go?"

"Of course." Kit reached for her keys hanging beside the cupboard and removed one from the ring.

Wren thanked her and said goodbye to both of them. When the front door closed behind her, Sarah said, "I'm not saying there hasn't also been good that's come out of all this. I know there are people that can be helped by hearing your story. But talking about mental illness is hard. You know that. And I just want to make sure you're aware of the potential of being judged and misunderstood, that you're willing to risk that."

Kit put an Earl Grey tea bag into each mug, then stared at the water boiling, waiting for the click of the switch. She was willing and ready. Wasn't she?

MARCH 3

My dear Wren,

It's often been the case that whatever I'm intending to present at a retreat has direct application to my own life. That was true this morning as I taught about temptation. There I was, having only just written to you a few days ago about being stripped of reputation or the need to defend myself, and all I was thinking about was how I might need to clarify or explain some of the details I shared last week from my own story. What if someone had misunderstood what I said? What if someone thought less of me because of the weaknesses and struggles I shared? What if, what if, what if.

I told you, I'll never be free this side of heaven of my desire for control. But—by the grace of God—I was able to resist the temptation and let the words I spoke last week stand on their own. No doubt the temptation will rise again. That's the thing about temptation. It always seeks "an opportune time."

As I thought today about all the many ways Jesus was tempted, not just in the desert but during his ministry and at the cross, I remembered the detail of the passersby and the authorities deriding him, demanding he demonstrate he was the Son of God by coming down from the cross. Not only had Jesus refused to defend himself against false accusations, but here he also refused to prove his identity by using his power. What a temptation that must have been! Especially when the religious leaders claimed they would believe in him if he just came down.

But he remained. Thank God.

Their words pursue me tonight: "He trusts God. Let God deliver him."

I've heard a similar voice in my own life and in the lives of others. It's easy to believe the lie that the only testimony that can lead someone to

faith is the testimony of deliverance. We sometimes think the only testimony that will bring God glory is the testimony of victory. We can
even use deliverance and victory as a litmus test of God's trustworthiness.
Or—and I have been guilty of this plenty of times—we can use our
trust in God as a bargaining chip to obligate him to deliver us. As if
my faith could somehow obligate him to serve me on my own terms.
Lord, have mercy.

Jesus trusted in God. God did not deliver him from the cross. What a
profound and comforting mystery this is, that our suffering, too, can be a
testimony that reveals the truth of who Christ is. Our deaths can be rev-
elations of his life and power. Even if it's harder for others—and us—to see.

I think of his mother, standing there at the foot of the cross, watching
her son suffer, and listening to every vile insult hurled at him. I know how
I felt whenever anyone criticized or condemned my boy. I know how I felt,
watching him suffer and feeling powerless to do anything to help him. And
this is only an inkling of Mary's pain.

If I had been Mary, I would have joined in with the authorities and
begged him to come down and show everyone who he was. I would have
been remembering Gabriel's word of promise, declaring who my son
would be. I would have been remembering the shepherds testifying to the
angels singing at his birth. I would have been remembering the magi
kneeling to worship him. And I would have been wondering, "Is this how
it's meant to be?"

As Mary watched his anguish and felt her own, maybe she also remembered how Simeon had prophesied in the temple over her baby,
telling her a sword would pierce her heart too.

And then came that moment when, with labored breath, he spoke to
her from the cross: "Woman, behold your son." Maybe she thought, "Yes!

Yes! I'm beholding you, and my heart is breaking!" But when he next spoke to John, it became clear he was entrusting her to someone else's care. Such a beautiful act of love. But with such a ring of finality. As if, even if he rose from the dead as he'd promised—even if this evil was not the end of the story—he would no longer be her son in the way he had been before. And maybe her heart broke again.

There's a scene I wish had been recorded in the Gospels: the moment when Mary saw her resurrected son. What was that reunion like? I can only imagine the joy of embracing him again, of hearing his voice speak tenderly to her.

That's the scene I want to see because that's the scene I look forward to myself. Not only the moment of seeing Jesus face to face, but the moment of being reunited with my son, even as he will not be my son in the same way he was before. But he will be well. He will be whole. And I look forward to that day.

The sword of sorrow has pierced your heart too. You have already endured such profound grief and suffering. But your story also has the power to bring comfort and healing to others. Your life rings with the testimony of God's faithfulness. Even if it is not the testimony you would choose, it is beautiful. And it is yours to share.

With you,

Kit

11

It Is Finished

MARCH

"I think I may be nearing the end," Kit told Russell when they met for spiritual direction.

He sat forward in his chair. "The end of . . . ?"

"My active working life. My tenure at New Hope. It's been niggling at me the past six months, I guess. Not strong enough on my radar to think about it deeply, not with everything else going on. But I'm paying attention to the disequilibrium and unrest I'm feeling, and I'm open to the possibility that it's time for me to step aside and let new leadership emerge." She glanced out the window at swirling snow. "I'm tired, Russell. And I don't think it's just a physical tired."

He waited for her to say more.

She ran her hand slowly along the armrest of the couch. "I spoke to one of the board members yesterday and told her what I'm praying about. She didn't seem surprised. We've been together in discernment for the past few years, and neither of us has ever had a sense it was time for me to step away. Until now."

He was silent a moment, then said, "When you think about leaving New Hope, what happens in your spirit?"

She closed her eyes and imagined herself clearing out her office and turning in her key. "I feel sorrow. Like a good chapter is closing. But also relief. And gratitude."

The parts of her job she had loved most—leading retreats and offering spiritual direction—could continue in a different way. She could offer spiritual direction in her home. And New Hope hosted many events with other facilitators. She might still be able to lead her fall Sacred Journey retreat. Or facilitate the occasional workshop. If the Lord led her to do it.

She kept imagining each ending, each change. "The more I think about it, the more I feel peace. Without any twinge of regret." She opened her eyes again.

"That's an important observation," Russell said.

Yes. It was. She would need to test that movement of her soul, though, and make sure there wasn't something she was running from or ignoring. She would do what she had counseled others to do in discernment: make a nonbinding decision within herself and see if the sense of consolation deepened over the next few days. She would ask God for the gift of holy indifference, for the grace to choose whatever would bring him glory and honor and lead to his deepening life in her. She would ask him to deliver her from any fear that might cloud her listening. And she would ask him to guide her in joy.

She wove her fingers together in her lap. "I think the stirring is coming to the surface now because of something that happened during one of the retreat sessions a few weeks ago." As Russell listened attentively, she told him how she had sensed the Lord's invitation to share part of her story and how that had led to a difficult, forthright conversation with Sarah. "I told her we both need to have the freedom to steward our stories with truth and grace. And I reassured her that I would continue to honor her part of the story. That's hers to tell, if she chooses to." She breathed slowly. "I just want to make sure that in light of all this, I'm being led forward, not driven."

"Tell me more about that," he said.

Kit inhaled and exhaled slowly. "I want to be sure any potential negative fallout from my sharing at the retreat isn't driving my thoughts about leaving. Not that anyone on the board is concerned about what I shared or how I shared it. But I do wonder, going forward, what other possibilities might open for me to speak vulnerably about my experience with depression, once I'm not serving as the director there." She paused. "Honestly, leaving my job feels like both a culmination and a beginning."

"Like a birth," he said.

Yes, she thought. Like a birth. Or a death with a promise of resurrection.

Kit was working at her desk later that afternoon when there was a knock on the door. "Come in," she called.

Wren entered, a sheepish expression on her face. "Gayle said you were done with your meeting, so . . ."

"Right, it's fine." She set down her pen and pushed aside a stack of papers.

Wren held up her phone. "I may regret this later, but I just sent a text to Casey's mom."

Kit tried to conceal her surprise. "Did you?"

"I couldn't let it go. I felt like I wanted to at least explain that I didn't intend to cause them any hurt. Could I read you what I wrote?"

"Of course."

Wren sat down on the edge of a chair. "'Hi, Mrs. Wilson,'" she began, her voice soft. "'I'm really sorry you were upset when you found out we had a small memorial service to honor Casey. It was important for me to have a chance to say goodbye to my friend, and when my pastor offered to lead one, I said yes. I never intended to cause you or Brooke or the rest of the family any hurt.'" She looked up, as if seeking approval.

Kit nodded her encouragement.

Wren cleared her throat. "'Casey was like a brother to me. Even though I tried to love him well, I know sometimes I didn't express that love in good and healthy ways. Please tell Brooke I'm sorry for any harm I caused her by not wanting to let go of our friendship. I wish things could have been different. I wish there could have been a different ending for all of us. But even with all the pain, I'm so grateful for the gift of your son and his friendship in my life. And I pray God's comfort for all of you.'" She wiped her eyes. "And that's it. I was going to write a whole thing about how wonderful it was that people came to faith at the service, but that felt like I was trying to justify it. And I was worried that might make her angrier. I had a part in there, too, about praying for Estelle, but I deleted that. I deleted everything that sounded like I wanted something from them."

"That sounds very wise," Kit said.

"Dawn thought it was okay, sending it like it was. I guess I needed to try for closure and forgiveness. And if she doesn't reply, then I need to be okay with that somehow. I keep reminding myself I don't have control over how someone responds to me. I only have control over how I respond to others."

"You responded with grace and truth, Wren. I didn't hear anything accusatory or angry or defensive in what you wrote."

Wren looked up from her phone. "You don't think it was selfish of me, wanting to ask for forgiveness?"

"Why would that be selfish?"

"So they wouldn't be thinking hateful things about me. And so I wouldn't stay stuck."

Kit hoped her eyes communicated the tenderness she felt. "I love how you can even see that possibility and name it. That shows a lot of maturity." And far more discernment, she thought, than she'd had at Wren's age. "God can work through all our motivations—whether they're pure or a bit tainted—to move his kingdom forward. And I think you took a step in that direction today."

Wren glanced down again at her phone. "Thanks. I hope I don't become obsessed over getting a reply. I need to be able to let it go. I hope I can."

"You've done your part, dear one. You've said you're sorry. And you didn't frame it in a way that asked her to do anything for you in return. It's up to her now, whether she'll say yes to moving through her anger and bitterness or whether she'll be consumed by it. That's her choice." Not an easy choice, Kit thought, and one that Casey's mother would likely need to make many times as she journeyed through her grief. With her eyes still on Wren, Kit offered a silent prayer for the woman who had also lost a son.

Wren swiped her screen, then tucked her phone into her sweatshirt pocket. "Can I ask you something?"

"Sure."

She hesitated, then said, "What happened after Robert left?"

"In terms of the divorce, you mean?"

Wren sat back in the chair. "I mean, you talked about him having an affair with Carol and how you needed to work through your anger and bitterness, but you haven't written much about what happened between you after the divorce. Just that he died seven years ago."

Kit ran her hand slowly along the edge of her desk. "I was angry for a long time," she said. "Not just at Robert and Carol, but at God too. I felt betrayed. Like so many of the promises I'd believed about God weren't true. All those verses about him watching over and protecting the ones who trusted in him? Not allowing any harm to come to them? I'd tried to make sense of them during my work as a hospice chaplain. But what did those mean to me personally after Micah died? After my marriage died?

"And then one day a very wise counselor I was meeting with suggested I needed to forgive God, which sounded completely blasphemous to me. The more I thought about it, though, the more I realized that even if God didn't need my forgiveness, I needed to offer it. Or else I would forever harbor grudges against him and never fully entrust myself to his care. And I couldn't live like that."

"So, what did you do?"

She picked up her pen and clicked it. "I wrote God a letter. I offered him all my disappointment and named all my grievances in a raw, honest lament. The process of writing that letter and saying that I forgave him even if I didn't understand him cleared the air between us, and eventually I was able to move into a different kind of trust." She set her pen down again. "In many ways, the relationship I'd had with him before died, and there was no regaining it. Not to say that my relationship with him before all the heartache was better. In fact, I think I could safely say it's deeper now. Harder. But deeper. Like a married couple that's endured a fracture in their relationship and builds something even stronger because of it."

They shared the silence awhile, and then Wren said, "What about with Robert and Carol? What happened with them?"

Kit stared at the empty ring finger on her left hand. "I worked through a process of forgiveness on my own. Neither one of them ever said they were sorry. And that was hard. They moved to Arizona not long after they were married. Sarah sometimes went to visit them. She was able to keep a good relationship with her dad, and on my good days, I was glad about that. For her sake. She got along well with Carol too. And Carol became a beloved grandmother to my granddaughters. Which was also hard for me."

"I'm sorry," Wren said quietly. "Is she still in Arizona?"

"No, Florida now. She remarried, and Sarah says she's very happy." Kit sighed. "I wish I had a victory testimony to share with you about it. I wish I could say we all worked through a process of forgiveness and that we were able to reconcile with one another, maybe even that we were able to have a Christmas dinner together with the grandkids. But that never happened. When Robert died, Carol called Sarah to give her the news, and Sarah told me. She and her family flew out for the funeral." She paused. "And when all kinds of latent bitterness was suddenly tapped again in me, a wise friend suggested that perhaps I needed to forgive Robert for dying without saying he was sorry." That was something she had occasionally invited the bereaved families to do after a hospice patient died, to offer forgiveness and seek closure for any of the unresolved conflicts and hurts. But that was before she had a list of them herself. "It took a while," Kit said, "but I ended up writing Robert a letter too. And I buried it beside Micah's tombstone."

Wren was silent a long time. "I don't know if I've thought of this before," she finally said, "but I think maybe Casey was asking for my forgiveness. When he wrote the line about 'If you paint Jesus saying, Father, forgive them, think of me,' I thought maybe he was saying he was seeking God's forgiveness. But maybe he hoped for mine too." She looked at Kit. "I thought there would never be any closure for me after he died. But maybe there is. Even if it's not the kind I expected." She rose to her feet. "It's like you wrote in one of my letters, that we need to trust in the good ending for the whole story. Even if the chapters don't finish the way we want them to."

MARCH 11

My dear Wren,

I've been pondering one of Jesus' final words today: "It is finished."

What a glorious declaration. The work he had come to do, he had completed. He had purchased our salvation with his own blood. It was done. And no power of hell could make it come undone.

It is finished.

Those are words I need to keep rehearsing whenever I'm overwhelmed by all that is unfinished in this world and in my own life.

After my divorce was finalized, I bought the house you might remember (where you and your parents stayed for a few weeks when you first moved to America). Shortly after moving in, I decided I wanted more daylight in the family room, so I hired a company to put in a new window in a dark corner of the room and replace a couple of old windows on the side of the garage. The salesman told me ahead of time that I would need to stain the window frame when it was done, and I figured that wouldn't be difficult to do.

A few weeks later the installer came and cut through the wall. I was amazed by the daylight that poured into the room. While he was working, I ran some errands and got home as he was packing up his truck. He told me he'd come back the next day to replace the garage windows. I thanked him and went inside to enjoy my new view.

But what I saw when I turned the corner into the family room made me feel sick. Yes, the window was in. But the wall above it and around it had been cut right through. There were gaps and holes everywhere—a mess that was far more complicated to fix than what I had initially agreed to. I knew I would need to hire someone to repair the damage that had been done. And that would mean spending far more money than I had budgeted. I regretted ever deciding to put in the window.

That night I spiraled. That one visual mess brought to mind all the other messes and chaos and brokenness in my life and in the lives of people I loved. So I did the best thing I knew how to do: I lamented. I protested. I expressed to God my frustration and anger. I pleaded with him to be the God I know him to be, to show his faithfulness and intervene in the lives of those who were crying out in desperation for him.

The next morning the installer arrived. But instead of beginning his work on the garage, he brought tools and materials into the house. Over the next few hours he spackled, sanded, and repaired all the cracks, leaving only a small portion of wall that would need to be painted.

As I stood in front of my new window that night, I heard the Lord address me with three penetrating words: Let. Me. Finish.

I was silenced before him. Such a convicting and authoritative word. And a place for me to find rest.

I'm so quick to assume outcomes. Maybe that's one of the lasting wounds of my trauma: when I'm not spiritually attentive or when I'm physically tired, I mentally race to the worst possible ending. Hearing those three words that day shifted something in me. If I was going to let God finish his work, then I needed to practice waiting well. Waiting with patience and hope. Letting God be God and trusting him to fulfill his purposes. This, too, is part of lament. While we wait for God to act, we remember who he is and what he has done in the past so that we can trust him in the silence and hiddenness. We practice remembering. And we practice hope.

"It is finished," Jesus says. It's a bold declaration for us to make too. What does it mean to say "It is finished" when so much is unfinished? It means we are people who live hope in two directions, both backward and forward. We long for the kingdom to come in fullness, even as it has already come. And we trust that the One who has begun the good work in us and for us will indeed complete it.

With you,

Kit

12

Into Your Hands

MARCH

"I had no idea you'd made so much progress," Kit said, glancing around Wren's studio at bookshelves and windowsills displaying pencil and charcoal sketches of cups, hands in different positions, and a few unfinished paintings of faces.

"Most of them are just studies," Wren said. "I'm still trying to figure out what I can do and how to do it. And trying not to get discouraged in the process."

The Gethsemane one, with its central void, was propped against a stack of books on the table, the trees more brightly colored than before, splashed with some of Vincent's bright blue and citron yellow. "You didn't paint over it," Kit said.

Wren smiled wryly. "How could I, after what you saw in it?" She picked it up. "I've got to say how humbling it was, though, that what you noticed and what spoke to you in it wasn't something I'd intentionally created. That it was just an empty space. Nothing to do with me or my ability as an artist."

Kit placed her hand on Wren's back. "I'm sorry that's what I communicated to you."

"No, it's fine. That's what art does, right? It invites a response. And we can't control what people see or how they respond to what we create. To what I create." She shrugged. "Or don't create."

With her free hand Kit traced along the contours of the void. "You know what this says to me? This says you were listening. This says you weren't forcing your own will with the work, that you were waiting for it to emerge. And that you allowed the empty space to be—without trying to fill it."

Wren laughed. "You make me sound profound. But I would have tried to fill that space, if you hadn't caught me first." She set the piece back on the table and gestured toward a few canvases smeared with gray. "All those right there? Those were all my attempts at Gethsemane, all very poor copies of Vincent's olive trees, and all with a figure kneeling right in the center, with his head in his hands. But I couldn't capture the wrestling. I couldn't capture the agony. No matter how hard I tried. I knew it would be beyond me, and it was."

"Ah," Kit said quietly, "but you did capture the agony. You captured his presence by painting his absence. That's what I feel in the void there and in the empty space along the bottom—the invitation to wrestle, surrender, and yes, die. With him." She squeezed Wren's shoulder. "Be open to the possibility that the mystery of what emerged in this work mirrors your own journey, not just as an artist, but as a person. You're inhabiting these spaces with Jesus. And that's exactly what I hoped and prayed you would do."

Wren sighed slightly. "I'm still not convinced any of this is for anyone else. Maybe it's just been for me."

"Not just for you," Kit said. "For me too."

Wren picked at a bit of paint on her fingernail. "And maybe for my family," she said. "My mom called this morning. They're still planning to drive out here for spring break, if the weather cooperates. So I was wondering if it would be okay to put up the Journey to the Cross stations early so they can walk through them?"

"Of course!"

"I don't know what I'll have finished by then." She glanced around the room. "Some of these, I guess. I can keep working with these. And then if I decide to put out something different for the real journey—I mean, not the 'real' journey, but the open to the public one—I can change things around."

"We can make anything work," Kit said, "so, no pressure." As she took one last look at the Gethsemane painting, she noticed on the table a fanned stack of her letters beside open books of Vincent's work, a few dried sunflowers, and Casey's beanie. She gestured toward the tableau. "That looks very Vincent-esque."

Wren nodded. "I couldn't bear to throw the flowers out after the service. And then I remembered how Vincent painted dried ones, so I thought I might try it sometime too, though I could never paint sunflowers the way he did. It's like you could pick the seeds right out of his flowers, they're so real." She placed her hand on the stack of letters. "And these. I keep reading them again and again. I can't thank you enough for writing these for me."

"Thank *you*, Wren. I've told you before how grateful I am for the spaces opening in me because of your presence in my life. You and I, we're companions in sorrow. And also in hope." Kit stroked the tip of a sunflower stem. "I think Vincent would be proud of you. You're finding your own voice in all of this. And that's always brave."

As they put away dinner dishes that night, Wren said she'd been thinking about setting up a prayer collage for one of the stations, as an experiential way of meditating on a Scripture text. "But would that look weird, having one that's not a painting?"

"Not at all," Kit said. "We've had other interactive stations over the years." One of her favorites was a full-sized cross with a mirror angled at the center of the crossbeam so that someone kneeling in front of it could see their own reflection and ponder the meaning. "Which one are you thinking about?"

"Jesus speaking to the women weeping. I've been picturing the sorrow collages you did at your retreat and wondered about inviting people to glue or tape images onto the shape of a cross. They could choose photos from your files or cut out pictures or headlines from newspapers or magazines—anything that feels sad or overwhelming. But then there would be a community piece to it too—everyone placing the images on the cross to offer in prayer. So it's like what you wrote in one of your letters, how the community of sorrow can become the community of hope."

"It's perfect," Kit said. "A perfect way to pray with that text."

"Oh, good. If I can manage it, I'll look through headlines and see what catches my attention. There's plenty of sad to choose from these days."

"So true," Kit said. "You don't need to do that alone, though. We can do it together."

"Thanks. I'd like that." She checked her phone when it buzzed with a text, then put it back on the kitchen counter. "Every time it buzzes, I wonder if it'll be Casey's mom. But it never is. And probably won't ever be."

Kit studied her face, trying to discern her expression. Regret? Resignation? Or a peaceful surrender? "How do you feel about that?" she asked.

Wren shrugged. "I did what I thought was right to do. I've got to let the other desires go. Or, I guess I should say, keep letting them go."

Yes, Kit thought. Letting go was always the invitation. "Can you think of anything that might help with that? Maybe a physical embodiment of that desire?"

Wren thought a moment, then said, "I probably should delete the text she sent me. But I feel like that's too simple, like it doesn't leave enough of an imprint. I'm not sure if that makes sense."

Kit closed the cupboard doors and draped the dish towel over the rack. "I'd love to hear more about that."

Wren leaned back against the counter. "I think what I want to do is mark it somehow, to incorporate it as part of a larger picture of healing and forgiveness. Maybe I could copy and paste it into an email and print it, then shred it and use it in a collage. Or"—

here, her eyes widened—"print it and burn it and use the ashes in one of the Journey to the Cross paintings."

Before Kit could reply, Wren furrowed her brow and said, "Or would that be self-centered, making the art too therapeutic? I mean, I know we put ourselves into our work and work things through in the process of creating, but this might be a little much. I don't want to make the paintings about me. That feels selfish."

They were cut from the same cloth, the two of them. Kit was just about to remind Wren of the conversations they'd had over her own hesitation to share her story with others, for fear of calling too much attention to herself, when Wren said, "But maybe it's not. If I see it as an offering to Jesus, then it's not selfish, is it? It's a gift of myself. My raw and honest self. And maybe it's even something he can use to help someone else."

"I think it's a beautiful vision," Kit said.

Wren smiled slowly, her eyes lit. "There's something to it, isn't there? Like the ashes on our foreheads. A way of marking the journey forward by letting go of what lies behind."

Kit nodded and said, "Amen."

MARCH 13

My dear Wren,

I keep thinking about your idea of incorporating ashes into your work. It makes me wish I still had some of the angry letters I wrote and never sent, letters I threw away after the cathartic experience of writing them. I would have burned them and asked you to paint something redemptive for me as well. I wonder, too, why I felt compelled not to destroy my final "I forgive you" letter to Robert, but instead to bury it at Micah's grave. Maybe, like you so insightfully expressed, I needed to mark something solid and final with it and not just let it disappear.

After my divorce I desperately wanted a fresh start—which can be hard to attain in a community as small and interconnected as West Michigan. But I knew I needed to take a first step, so I gave up using my nickname Kit—which family and friends had always used—and started going by Katherine in new or professional contexts. I also started attending a different church, Church of the Redeemer. It was the art that first drew me there—something familiar for me to hold onto after my experience of praying with the stations of the cross at the psychiatric hospital. Some Sundays I would simply sit at the far end of the back pew, stare at the carving of Jesus before Pilate, and cry.

It must have been the first service of the new year, nearly two years after Micah died, that the pastor invited us to write on slips of paper sins we wanted to confess or regrets and shame we wanted to release. I don't remember now what I would have written, but I joined the line of others who walked to the front of the sanctuary to place our slips of paper at the foot of the cross. After the service, without reading them, the pastor gathered all the slips into a single manila envelope, and we went out to the church parking lot to watch them burn. He lined an ordinary stock pot with aluminum foil, placed the envelope in the pot, and lit a match. As the envelope burned, I happened to notice the shadow of the pot, which had somehow elongated into the shape of a pillar with a dome on top, with the shadows of the smoke rising from it, swirling on the pavement. It looked like an altar. I don't know if anyone else noticed it—and I wish now that I had thought to call someone else's attention to it—but it spoke to me deeply and personally, that the releasing of our sins, regrets, and shame was a pleasing offering to the Lord.

After the envelope burned, the pastor carefully gathered up all the ashes and said they would be incorporated into our ashes for Ash Wednesday. It was a meaningful experience for us when we went forward that year to receive on our foreheads the reminder of the price Jesus paid for our forgiveness and freedom. Exactly as you said: that we mark the journey forward by letting go of what lies behind.

Most years—weather permitting—we gather after our Palm Sunday service, palm branches in hand, and march outside waving them. Then we lay them on a bonfire. This, too, is powerful imagery—that all of the expectations we carry with us of who Jesus is as a conquering king and mighty warrior are laid down as we enter into the mysteries of Holy Week and the reality of the cross. It's all part of the journey. The cross not only rightly reorients our hopes and longings, but ultimately accomplishes far more glorious victories than any of the pilgrims who waved their branches along the road to Jerusalem could have imagined. Every year when I lay down my palm branch in the fire, I try to practice the discipline of laying down my assumptions about what victory looks like in my life or in the lives of those I love.

"It is finished!" Jesus called from the cross. But he also prayed, "Into your hands I commit my spirit." This is the ultimate modeling both of letting go and declaring hope. What a beautiful prayer of relinquishment and trust. For all of us.

I look forward with eager anticipation to see how the ashes in your life will become an image of beauty and a testimony of hope and redemption—not just for you, but for others.

With you,

Kit

13

Buried

MARCH

A few days before Jamie, Dylan, and the kids were scheduled to arrive from North Carolina, Wren was ready to call them and tell them not to come. "They haven't started driving yet," she told Kit in her office. "There's still time for me to say I can't manage the stress."

Kit folded her hands on her desk. "What about it feels most stressful to you?"

"Everything." Wren paced back and forth. "I still don't even know which paintings I can use, and I feel like I'll lose days of preparing for the real event by trying to entertain them. I love my family and everything, but Phoebe can get really clingy and demanding, and I don't have time or energy for that right now."

Kit had never met the littlest Crawford—and she hadn't seen the older kids since they were in elementary school—but she knew from Dylan and Jamie that Phoebe could be a challenge. "It sounds like they have lots of other plans while they're out here," she said, "between Olivia's college tours and their trip to Chicago."

"Yes, but I think they're hoping I'll go with them to Chicago. And that's the last thing I need right now."

"So, say that."

Wren stopped pacing and sighed. "I've already disappointed them so often the past few months. Every time I talk with Phoebe, she mentions me not being there for Thanksgiving and Christmas. I feel like I should try to make it up to her."

In the silence, Sarah's words returned, how Morgan and Jess had been disappointed by her absence at Christmas. "We're dust, remember?" Kit said. "We've got physical and emotional and psychological limits. Your parents will understand, even if Phoebe doesn't. Maybe you could do something special with her while she's here. Take her to Kingsbury Gardens to see the butterflies. I bet she'd love that. My granddaughters always did when they were younger."

Wren appeared to be considering this.

"And as far as the paintings go," Kit said, "put out what you can. I'll write reflection questions for whatever stations you decide to do. And it will be a beautiful journey of prayer. The Spirit will bring it all to life." *Remember, it's not about you,* Kit wanted to say, but didn't. Instead, she said, "I know you didn't want to look at the other art so you wouldn't be influenced"—she didn't say the word, *intimidated*— "but you might feel better if you really know that the pressure's off." Wren stared at her. "So, what do you say? Want to have a look?"

Wren nodded slowly. "Okay."

A few hours later Kit found Wren kneeling on the floor in the chapel, surrounded by paintings from other artists. "I've found one I definitely want to use," she said, and gestured toward a favorite of Kit's: a painting of Jesus, arms extended as though he were still hanging from the cross. But no cross was visible. Instead, the bright colors and explosion of light around him testified to his victory over the grave. In a single painting the artist had managed to capture both his sacrifice and his resurrection. "This could be the one for 'It is finished,' don't you think?"

"Yes, it would be great for that."

"There's so much hope and confidence in this," Wren said. "It's the sort of painting I need to keep sitting with, the kind I know I'm not ready to paint. And if I use it, I need to get over myself and let my work be what it is, without measuring or comparing it against something like this."

"That sounds like a wonderful discipline to practice," Kit said.

Wren sat back on her knees. "Another dying, right? I've got to let go of my own expectations and try to focus on doing this as prayer and worship." She gave Kit a wry smile. "Guess I'll never run out of things to relinquish."

"Well, look how much older I am than you, and I haven't found the end of it yet. The circumstances change, but many of the underlying issues remain." Kit paused. "I don't say that to discourage you. If anything, I'm saying, Don't be discouraged by the process. It is what it is. We just keep offering our yes."

"And let go of the outcome," Wren said quietly.

"Right."

Wren rose to her feet and brushed off her jeans. "I've done a few more paintings, if you're interested in seeing them. I mean, they're not finished, but . . ."

Kit smiled at her. "Or maybe they are," she said, and followed Wren to the studio.

While Wren was out with Mara that evening, Kit sat with her lit Christ candle, a blank pad of paper in front of her. Perhaps before writing any formal letter of resignation to the board, there was one more step of prayer for her to take. *Katherine Rhodes, age 75*, she wrote at the top of the page, *left her role as director of the New Hope Retreat Center on*—she paused. When might she leave it? What would best serve the ministry? Try to hold on to another set of programming in the fall, or let go early enough for them to reenvision what autumn might look like without her?

She pulled out her calendar and scanned the upcoming commitments. Once the Lenten retreat was over, there were only guest facilitators scheduled to lead events through the spring and summer. All of them had been leading workshops and retreats at New Hope for many years. It wouldn't be difficult for someone to oversee the coordination of their needs. And if the board wanted her to remain part time for a while to help with a transition, she could do that. That was how she had originally transitioned into her role as the director: after leading the fall Sacred Journey retreats for a few years and offering other workshops as she was able, she had discerned a call to leave the ministry of chaplaincy to say yes to full-time work at New Hope.

It was time to let go.

She thumbed through the calendar again. Easter would be too soon to give notice. Or would it? She had already mentioned to the board that she was prayerfully considering the timing of her departure. Perhaps she could present her formal resignation the week after Easter and then let the board decide what work they wanted her to continue to do.

Or . . .

She traced her finger over one particular date: March 31. The thirty-sixth anniversary of Micah's death. And this year, Holy Saturday, the day of hope mingled with sorrow, the day of keeping watch to see what might rise from the dead. That was her day to write the letter and let go.

The front door opened and closed. Wren called her greeting. Kit called back, then quietly tore the piece of paper from the pad and tucked it underneath as Wren rounded the corner.

"Good time with Mara?" Kit asked.

"She's wonderful. There's nothing false about her. That's why I love having her look at my work. She'll tell me if it's crap."

Kit laughed. "Yes, she will. And did she?"

"No. She says I'm the one who's full of it and that it would be selfish of me not to put out what I've done so that other people can pray with it." She unwound her scarf. "She did say my painting of Jesus was ugly, though."

Kit raised her eyebrows. She had seen it in Wren's studio that day: a haunting image of the Man of Sorrows keeping silent before his accusers.

"She didn't say it in a mean way," Wren said. "It was just the first thing she blurted out when she saw it."

Kit could imagine Mara doing so and suppressed a smile.

"Casey used to say the same exact thing about Vincent's portraits," Wren went on, "so I guess I could take it as a compliment. I was trying to capture the essence of Jesus' spirit and the meaning of that moment instead of doing something literal. That's what Vincent wanted to do with the people he painted." She fiddled with the tassels on her scarf. "Anyway, it ended up speaking to Mara, and she couldn't stop staring at it. So I guess that's something. And if I incorporate ashes into it, I guess that could make it even more meaningful. To me, at least."

Kit rested her elbows on the kitchen table and clasped her hands together. "I think that's a powerful vision, Wren. And as for the painting being 'ugly,' I'd say it's compelling. It's like Isaiah says, that there was no majesty or beauty to attract us to him, that he was oppressed and afflicted. To me, your painting expresses Jesus' solidarity with us. And I love that it's not a traditional image of him. I hope you'll keep it."

"I'll keep working with it, anyway," Wren said, "and see where it goes."

Kit decided not to press her. Let the Spirit do his work.

Wren clutched her scarf to her chest. "I was thinking about something else while I was out," she said, "how I need to write a forgiveness and goodbye letter to Casey. At first I thought I could burn it and use the ashes in the Jesus painting. But the more I thought about it, the more I realized I don't want it mixed with his mother's text. I want to give it a proper burial, and not in a random place. So I wondered if it would be okay to do it at New Hope. In the courtyard garden."

Kit was too surprised to reply.

"I know there are already lots of flowers planted there, so I got to thinking, what if I took the sunflower seeds from Casey's flowers and planted them? Then it would be a sort of memorial, even if it's temporary. A tribute to Vincent too."

"It's a beautiful idea, Wren."

"It would be okay, then? Burying the letter and planting the seeds out there?"

"Of course."

Wren thanked her. "New Hope was the last place Casey and I were together. It's where he was thinking about Jesus and where he made some important decisions, whatever they were. I'll have to bury my unknowing about all that too." She gazed out a window, her pensive expression reflecting in the glass. "I'm not ready to write it yet. I'm not sure when I will be. But if I've got something meaningful to do with the letter after I've written it, I think it will help me say the hard things I need to say."

Kit stared at the smoke curling upward from the Christ candle and offered a silent prayer for her. The day Wren could name the truth about the hurt Casey had caused and the ways he had deceived her would be a significant milestone in her journey of grief.

"I've read his goodbye letter so often," Wren said, "I've memorized it. There's that line where he says that if I paint the thief on the cross—the one who said he was sorry—I could paint his face and think of him. I'm not ready to do anything like that. I might never be. But when I was reading that story today, it struck me that maybe I've been interpreting that part of his note wrong. Because even though the thief knew his own guilt, he turned to Jesus and said, 'Remember me.' Like even though he knew what he deserved, he had hope. Maybe Casey was telling me that. Not only asking me to remember him, but telling me he'd asked Jesus to remember him too."

Aware of the lump rising in her throat, Kit smiled gently at her.

Wren smiled back. "You know what? I actually caught myself being happy today. And immediately felt guilty about it. Then it was as if I heard Casey's voice again, chiding me and telling me to get over myself and move on because *he* has. Don't get me wrong. I'd give anything to have Casey back. But today it was like I finally embraced the possibility of having him present in a different way. If that makes sense."

Kit nodded and rose to embrace her.

MARCH 17

My dear Wren,

Today, after leading the Lenten retreat, I spent time in my office reading the obituaries I wrote a couple of months ago for my marriage, my identity as Robert's wife, and my identity as Micah's mother. Even though these things died many years ago, I think there's something important about embalming them with love and gratitude and giving them a proper burial. It's not that I haven't already seen evidence of resurrection life after all these deaths. I have. But the act of naming the deaths is an invitation to name and remember the resurrections too.

As I write to you, I'm remembering our conversation about writing an obituary for our need for closure. I mentioned to you in an earlier letter that Micah's death was deemed "accidental." Though I suppose there was no way to know for sure, I gripped that word as a lifeline while I fought to recover. Psychologically, I couldn't bear the thought that it was otherwise. Sometimes, in the face of mystery, we have to give ourselves the ending we need in order to move forward.

There came a time—eventually—when I was well enough to entertain the possibility that Micah couldn't bear to live the life he'd been given and that the drugs he'd used to self-medicate were the ones he used to deliberately end his pain. People might say, Why does it matter? Your son is dead. Yes, and knowing for sure how and why he died doesn't change a thing about that.

But here's what I discovered: the closure I'd tried to bring by telling myself the version of the story that was easier to bear wasn't a strong enough seal against the unresolved questions, guilt, or regret that pursued me. I had to offer the Lord my need for closure about Micah's death. So, I guess in a way I did write that obituary years ago, though I didn't frame it like that at the time. All I knew was that I needed to bury that haunting mystery in the tomb of unknowing and then roll the stone into place so I wouldn't continue to be tormented by "if only" and "what if." Not that those weedy phrases don't rise up in new, ugly, and invasive ways in other places and circumstances. But we can become quicker at discerning them and plucking them out.

Someday all the mysteries of this life will be solved. But will that really matter when we see how thoroughly life has swallowed up death? When the tomb is finally opened and we see that it truly is empty, will any of the unresolved details matter?

Still, as long as we remain in these earthly bodies, we offer God our questions. We offer all our sorrow and bewilderment. We trust that our groans rise as fragrant incense before the throne of God. And we ask Jesus to catch and hold our tears.

I'm glad you're thinking about what kind of goodbye letter to write to Casey. I'm glad you're giving prayerful attention to a meaningful burial, combined with the hope of resurrection. In the face of an unexpected death, we're often so numb and overwhelmed, we can hardly manage the details of burial. That's why these other later burials can be so significant—an opportunity to be awake and reverent and aware of God's presence with us as we begin to realize all the other losses contained in the one death.

I picture the rush of Jesus' friends, trying to remove his body from the cross and bury him before the Sabbath began. I imagine the agony of the women, already distraught at laying him in the tomb, their distress exacerbated by the reality that they couldn't embalm him as they desired and as he deserved. There was no time to lovingly anoint him. It was all too sudden. Too hurried. In the hours that followed, including the dark hours of Holy Saturday, they weren't thinking that they would find an open and empty tomb when they returned. They were only thinking that they would have time to weep, mourn, and say their final goodbyes. But their grieving was suddenly and gloriously interrupted when they saw him face to face. So it will be with us someday.

I look forward to a spring day together, long after the danger of frost has passed, when you and I will kneel to bury and plant. And I look forward to a summer day when those dazzling golden orbs, their heavy heads mirroring the sun and tracking its movement across the sky, remind us of the irrepressible power of Life.

With you,

Kit

14

Risen

MARCH

Wren rubbed her brow as Kit surveyed the paintings lined up side by side in the New Hope chapel. "We can choose some from the other artists if these aren't good enough," she said. "I mean, after my family walks through, we can change them."

Before Kit could reply with reassurance—again—Wren picked up her painting of Jesus stretched out on the cross, his mother slumped over beneath his feet, the sword of grief and anguish piercing her heart. Standing alongside, the beloved disciple reached to steady and embrace her. "People are going to wonder why I painted birds around him and why it's light around him instead of darkness, like it's supposed to be. I still have time to change it, I think. My family won't be here for another couple of hours. I could paint over the birds, and it'll dry in time." She clutched the painting to her chest.

Kit gently pried it from her and set it back on the easel. "Why did you paint the birds?"

Wren was silent a long time. Then she said, "Because it seemed like they belonged. Like witnesses."

"Then they belong," Kit said. "They emerged from your prayer and imagination, so they belong."

"But they might be distracting for someone else."

"Then let them be distracting and let people prayerfully ponder why they're distracted." Kit smiled at her. "As for me, what comes to mind as I look at them is the Emily Dickinson line, 'Hope is the thing with feathers.' It makes me think of what you said about that painting there"—she pointed to the one Wren had chosen by the other artist for the "It Is Finished" station—"and how you said you weren't ready to paint that kind of hope or victory. But I see hope and faith in yours too—gentle and vulnerable and tentative and resilient—how you've juxtaposed the intense sorrow with the promise of resurrection in the flight of these birds. Even if the ones who are overcome with grief can't see it."

Wren pointed to a figure on the left side of the painting, who was gazing upward. "She sees it."

Kit shifted her gaze from the grieving mother to the robed woman whose eyes were fixed on Jesus' face. Or perhaps she was watching the birds in their wordless witness. "You're right," Kit said. "She sees it."

Wren pressed her hands to her heart. "I think she's me," she said quietly. "I didn't realize it until just now. But I think she's me, looking up at the Man of Sorrows. Identifying with him. So grateful for him. But also seeing that it's not the end of the story. The suffering, the sorrow—that's not the end." She reached out and touched the blue bird above the woman's head. "And I think the bird might be me too. I think I subconsciously put myself in both places." She laughed. "How could I have missed something so obvious? It's even blue, like the blue fairywren I was named after."

Kit laughed too. "Well, I didn't make the connection either. But what a beautiful gift from the Spirit, Wren. After so many losses and so much sorrow, you're moving into hope. Into resurrection."

Wren tilted her head, eyes still fixed on the painting. "Okay," she said after a moment, "that one can stay, but what about"— she reached for the one beside it, a painting of a chalice she had done for the "Jesus Is Crucified" station—"I'm not sure whether this one actually fits here or whether I should—"

"Tell you what," Kit said, placing her hand on Wren's. "I've got an idea. How about if we go out for an 'It is finished' celebration lunch before your family arrives?"

Wren hesitated. Then she straightened the painting on its easel, brushed a speck of dust from the canvas, and stepped back for one final look. "I guess it belongs," she said. "I guess it all belongs."

"It does, indeed," Kit replied, and walked with her to the car.

"She did it," Jamie murmured to Kit from the back corner of the chapel.

"Yes, she did," Kit said. "And she did it beautifully."

Jamie's brow relaxed as she scanned the room. "I wasn't sure she would be able to, not without it taking her under again."

There had been moments, Kit thought, when she hadn't been sure either. But she wasn't going to admit that. "She's a brave girl, Jamie."

"You're right," Jamie said. "She is."

At the front of the chapel, Wren was kneeling with Phoebe, explaining to her about how to choose pictures for the sorrow and hope collage, while Dylan, Joel, and Olivia made their way slowly around the room.

"Do you really think this will be your last one?" Jamie asked, her voice still low.

Kit shrugged. "I hope they'll keep the tradition going after I retire, but that will be out of my hands." It was another relinquishment to make, letting go of the observances that had been meaningful for her. "Wren is going to help me get art on the walls so that I'll leave here having given the physical space a more intentional, prayerful feel."

"She mentioned that to me," Jamie said. "And as far as leaving this place with your mark on it, I don't think you have any idea how many lives you've touched by being here and doing what you do."

"Thank you. It's been an honor and a delight." Kit watched as Wren and Phoebe began cutting out pictures together. "I told Wren the other day that even though there will be a new director sometime in the next few months, it seems to me that she'd be able to continue here part time if she wants to, unless they do a lot of restructuring. And as for where to live, she can stay with me as long as she needs to. We'll continue to be prayerful about that and see what God has in mind."

"Thank you so much, Kit. She seems well. Like she's reached a place of equilibrium again. I guess I worry about what more upheaval could do to her. But I need to let that go." Jamie gestured toward the first prayer station, Gethsemane. "And speaking of letting go, that looks like the perfect place to practice."

"I'll join you there," Kit said. With her hand resting on Jamie's shoulder for balance, she removed her shoes.

That night, after Jamie and the family left the house, Wren entered the kitchen carrying a vase filled with sunflowers. "These are for you," she said, handing them to Kit.

"For me?"

"As a very small token of appreciation. For everything you've done for me." Wren kissed her on the cheek. "I thought it might be nice if you had some seeds to plant in the New Hope courtyard too."

Kit lowered her face into the flowers, the petals soft against her skin. "What a thoughtful gift, Wren. Thank you."

"You're welcome." Wren poured herself a glass of water. "I'm wondering if you can do without me the next few days. I'll get the cleaning done in the morning, but then I think I might join my family on their trip to Chicago."

"I think that's great."

"You're sure? I can be back by Friday and clean up before the retreat on Saturday."

"No, don't come back early for that. It'll be fine, no worries." Kit set the vase on the kitchen table and sat down, motioning for Wren to join her.

"When I told Phoebe there's a huge art museum in Chicago," Wren said, "she got really excited. They've got a whole room full of Vincent's paintings, and I haven't seen them in years. So it should be a fun field trip together."

"I'm glad you're going."

Wren smiled. "It occurred to me it's probably best if I'm not here fretting over what I could paint or change for the stations. I need to leave them as they are for Holy Week."

"That sounds very wise," Kit said.

"Well, I don't know about wisdom, but it helps with my anxiety." She took a sip of water. "And speaking of that, I've been talking with Dawn for a while now about going back to work full time. I've had plenty of time to rest and recover—without pressure— and I know that's a luxury most people like me don't have. I also know I couldn't have done it without your generosity, letting me live here."

Kit leaned forward in her chair. "This is your home, Wren. For as long as you want or need it to be."

"Thank you. That means a lot to me."

"No shame in it either," Kit said. "I know people joke about their adult kids living in their basements, but for some of us, living on our own isn't all it's cracked up to be. I don't know why we equate maturity or health with being able to live independently, especially when living in community can be such a gift. I don't say that to pressure you, but just to say that your being here is a blessing to me too."

Wren reached across the table and clutched Kit's hand. "But you'll tell me, won't you, if it becomes a burden to you? If I become a burden? You'll be honest with me?"

"I will," Kit said. She would have another honest conversation with Sarah too, and if Sarah continued to express concern over Wren not moving on, Kit would invite Sarah to be open to the possibility that what she thought was best for her mother might not be. But there was no point having that conversation until things were more settled. Or until Sarah brought it up again. "I want you to be honest with me too, Wren. We'll be honest with each other."

"Okay. Deal." She squeezed Kit's hand before letting go. "So, about the work thing. I've got some applications out for everything from barista to office jobs. I know I might not find anything full time right away, but I definitely need to boost my weekly hours, even if it means working multiple part-time jobs. I feel like I can do that. I need to do that. I need to find a way to move forward." Wren stared at her lap. "I know I can't go back to social work, even if I wanted to. No agency would have me, not given my mental health history. I'd be a huge liability. So that door is permanently closed."

Kit shrugged slightly. "*Never* is a funny word with God."

Wren looked up at her.

"I thought the same thing after my breakdown," Kit said, "that I'd never be able to return to chaplaincy work. And it was true that hospice chaplaincy was no longer a good fit for me or the patients. Working solely with the dying and the bereaved was too much for me. But that didn't mean I didn't have a call to the ministry of compassion. And in fact, my own struggles and heartaches shaped me even more deeply for that work. So when it came time to interview for an opening at St. Luke's, I was very honest with them about what I'd been through. I told them I was committed to remaining in regular therapy and spiritual direction. And when they realized how aware I was of the potential triggers, they decided I would be a good fit for their team. As much as possible, I didn't work with adolescent patients unless there was an emergency—and sometimes there was. I won't say I prayed harder then—I tried always to be in prayer, no matter what situation I was in—but I was mindful afterward about any special care I might need."

She stared at the sunflowers, remembering with gratitude the people who had recognized her call and supported her as she lived it. That would be her ongoing prayer for Wren, that she would have everything she needed for becoming who she was created to be. No more. No less.

Kit smiled at her. "All this to say, I learned again through that process that the only 'never' we can say is, we can never be sure how God will work his purposes out. We just keep saying our next yes to whatever he reveals. And offer our surprise and grateful astonishment whenever things we counted as dead come to life again."

MARCH 31

My dear Wren,

Words can't express how proud I am of you, not only for persevering and painting your way through your grief, but also for relinquishing your work to the Lord so that he could speak to others through it. Many people talked to me this week about the impact the journey had on them and how your art helped them see something new about Jesus and his fierce love for us. Thank you for saying yes. You've said so many brave yeses along the way. And I know you'll say many more.

Today, during our silence and solitude retreat, I took time to write my letter to the board. My soul was already tender, remembering Micah today, and that, combined with the official relinquishing of work I have loved, meant there were quite a few tears to shed. But it was healing and good to mark this new transition on a day that was already important to me, not only because of Micah but also because of the convergence with Holy Saturday. This is the day of waiting, grieving what we've lost while we're not yet sure what will rise in its place.

Resurrection never comes as we expect. I think of Mary Magdalene weeping at the tomb, new grief layered upon fresh sorrow. Jesus isn't where they left him! Now what? Then, even when she sees him and is overcome with joy and relief, he tells her not to cling to him. If I had been Mary, I don't think I would have obeyed. If I thought I'd lost him once, only to get him back, I don't think I would have easily let him go again. And yet, letting go always sits at the core of our journeys, painful as it is.

I've been thinking today, too, about how grief and bewilderment can veil our sight and keep us from noticing the ways Jesus does appear with resurrection life. For Mary, she didn't recognize him until he spoke her name. The disciples on the road to Emmaus didn't recognize him until he took the bread and broke it for them. Thomas needed to see his wounds. And I've needed the gift of community to help me see his presence in the midst of desolation. Even then, it's often only in retrospect that I glimpse how he has kept me company, as he did—incognito—with the heart-broken, disappointed disciples trudging their way to Emmaus from Jerusalem. He gently asks questions, refuses to rush me to joy, and opens the Word to reveal the mystery of God's providence. Often, only in retrospect do I see how my own heart burned with recognition, even when my mind did not—or could not—perceive him.

And so, dear one, we keep watch in all the gardens where we've planted our sorrow, and we wait to see what he will do. What a gift to keep watch and wait in hope together.

With you,

Kit

Epilogue

A few days after Easter, Kit found Wren in the New Hope chapel, sitting on the chair she'd marked as Casey's and staring at her phone. Wren looked up when she heard footsteps. "I got a job," she said, gesturing to the screen. Before Kit could reply, she said, "It's only part time, but it's something. And I can start next week."

Kit studied her face, trying to discern whether this was news to be celebrated. "Where is it?" she asked.

"At a nursing home. It's a cleaning job—which will no doubt be far more intense than the cleaning here—but I liked the description of what they're trying to do for their residents, so I decided to apply. It's set days, set hours, so I can keep working here. And I think that will be enough for now, enough to get a handle on my expenses, get my student loans out of deferment, that sort of thing." Her eyes filled with tears. "Sometimes I wonder if I did the right thing, quitting my job at Bethel House. But I know I couldn't have kept going. I couldn't manage the stress." She pointed to her phone again. "I hope I can manage it there. If I fail at mopping floors and cleaning toilets . . . "

Kit sat down beside her and stared at her painting of the cross and the birds, which she had persuaded Wren to hang on the wall. "Well, we can both practice living into new things," Kit said. "Together."

Wren turned to face her. "You talked to the board?"

"Yes, a little while ago. They'd like me to stay on through the summer while they look for my replacement, and then I'll lead one last Sacred Journey retreat in the fall. Just the retreat, though— no more administrative duties after August. I've given them some names of people I think would do a wonderful job here, so we'll see what happens."

Wren leaned her head against Kit's shoulder. "It's like you've said in your letters. We just keep saying our next yes and trust God with all the deaths and resurrections."

Kit gazed out the far window at a courtyard still covered in snow, then closed her eyes to imagine the two of them kneeling side by side in the dirt to bury. And to plant.

JOURNEY
to the
CROSS

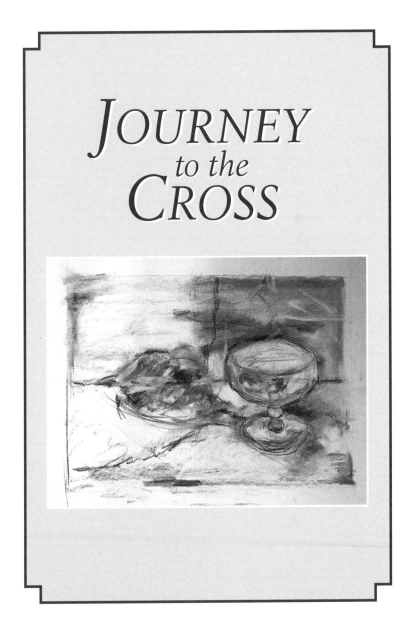

WELCOME TO JOURNEY TO THE CROSS. You are invited to accompany Jesus in his sorrow and suffering as he journeys from Gethsemane to Golgotha. As you explore the eight prayer stations, imagine you are watching the scenes unfold. Experience the details as you read the Scripture texts. Then read the artist statements and study the artwork. Try to move beyond judgment questions of, Do I like this? or Is it good?, and instead ask, What catches my attention? What thoughts, emotions, or memories are stirred in me as I view this? What attracts? What repels? Why? Seek to look through and beyond the art to the truth it illuminates. What invitations do you discern? How will you respond?

In the booklet you'll also find a section with reflection questions and prayer prompts for each station. Feel free to use whatever is helpful for you as you seek to enter the narrative. We hope you'll continue to ponder and pray with these Scripture texts throughout the year.

May the Lord lead you into the depths of his love as you walk with him.

Katherine Rhodes and Wren Crawford

REFLECTION GUIDE

STATION ONE
JESUS IN GETHSEMANE: MARK 14:32-42

Artist statement: "Pressed"

Gethsemane is a place of contrasts: terror and beauty, anguish and comfort, wrestling and surrender, absence and presence. Through color, form, and void, I sought to convey these polarities and reveal Jesus' solidarity with us in all our places of pressing and sorrow. What challenges or comfort do you find here?

They went to a place called Gethsemane; and he said to his disciples, "Sit here while I pray." He took with him Peter and James and John, and began to be distressed and agitated. And he said to them, "I am deeply grieved, even to death; remain here, and keep awake." And going a little farther, he threw himself on the ground and prayed that, if it were possible, the hour might pass from him. He said, "Abba, Father, for you all things are possible; remove this cup from me; yet, not what I want, but what you want." He came and found them sleeping; and he said to Peter, "Simon, are you asleep? Could you not keep awake one hour? Keep awake and pray that you may not come into the time of trial; the spirit indeed is willing, but the flesh is weak." And again he went away and prayed, saying the same words. And once more he came and found them sleeping, for their eyes were very heavy; and they did not know what to say to him. He came a third time and said to them, "Are you still sleeping and taking your rest? Enough! The hour has come; the Son of Man is betrayed into the hands of sinners. Get up, let us be going. See, my betrayer is at hand." (Mark 14:32-42)

▶ Ponder the words that describe Jesus' emotions in Gethsemane. Does anything surprise you? Challenge you? Comfort you? Why?

▶ Which details from the scene stir your thoughts, memories, or emotions?

  ● Are there any particular ways you can identify with Jesus?

  ● With the disciples?

▶ *Gethsemane* means "the oil press" or "the place of pressing oil." Consider all the ways Jesus is being pressed in this place.

  • What gifts do you receive as you watch and pray here?

▶ What does Jesus model for you in the garden? What do you learn from Jesus as he prays?

▶ Speak with God about what you have noticed during your time of reflection.

STATION TWO
JESUS IS BETRAYED BY JUDAS: MATTHEW 26:47-50

Artist statement: "Handed Over"

We use our hands to bless and wound, reject and serve, love and betray. In this self-portrait, I contemplate my own contradictions, seeing in the shadows my likeness to Judas and recognizing (with streaks and stains like tears) the ways I have handed myself over to greed, fear, and self-protection rather than handing myself over to love. What do you see?

While he was still speaking, Judas, one of the twelve, arrived; with him was a large crowd with swords and clubs, from the chief priests and the elders of the people. Now the betrayer had given them a sign, saying, "The one I will kiss is the man; arrest him." At once he came up to Jesus and said, "Greetings, Rabbi!" and kissed him. Jesus said to him, "Friend, do what you are here to do." Then they came and laid hands on Jesus and arrested him. (Matthew 26:47-50)

▶ Let the scene play out like a short movie in your imagination. Which details catch your attention? Stir your thoughts, memories, or emotions? Why?

▶ Place yourself in the scene in Gethsemane. How do you respond when Judas approaches? What do you try to do? What do you wish Jesus would do? Why?

▶ The Greek word for "betray" (*paradidomi*) is the same word used for "hand over." Bring to mind occasions when you have betrayed Jesus, others, or yourself and your principles. Recall moments when you have "handed yourself over" to sin.

  • Is there anything for you to confess and receive grace for?

▶ Bring to mind occasions when you have been betrayed by a friend or loved one. What was that experience like for you?

  • How does Jesus keep you company in this?

▶ Speak with God about what you have noticed during your time of reflection.

STATION THREE
PETER DENIES JESUS: LUKE 22:54-62

Artist statement: "Awakened"

In this painting I sought to capture the juxtaposition of despair and hope, failure and mercy—to communicate an invitation for us to be awake and hear the truth about our brokenness, not as a siren of condemnation but as a herald of grace. What does the rooster's crow signify to you?

Then they seized him and led him away, bringing him into the high priest's house. But Peter was following at a distance. When they had kindled a fire in the middle of the courtyard and sat down together, Peter sat among them. Then a servant-girl, seeing him in the firelight, stared at him and said, "This man also was with him." But he denied it, saying, "Woman, I do not know him." A little later someone else, on seeing him, said, "You also are one of them." But Peter said, "Man, I am not!" Then about an hour later still another kept insisting, "Surely this man also was with him; for he is a Galilean." But Peter said, "Man, I do not know what you are talking about!" At that moment, while he was still speaking, the cock crowed. The Lord turned and looked at Peter. Then Peter remembered the word of the Lord, how he had said to him, "Before the cock crows today, you will deny me three times." And he went out and wept bitterly. (Luke 22:54-62)

▶ Though Jesus had predicted that Peter would deny him, Peter had argued that he would never fall away. Have you, like Peter, ever denied your own capacity for failure? Bring to mind occasions when you were blind to your own weaknesses and pride.

  • What awakened you and convicted you? How did you respond?

▶ Are you prone to despair when you fail? What helps you return to Jesus?

▶ Imagine the scene in the courtyard. What is the expression on Jesus' face as he looks at Peter?

  • What is Jesus' expression as he looks at you?

▶ What kind of prayer do you need right now?

▶ Speak with God about what you have noticed during your time of reflection.

STATION FOUR
JESUS IS JUDGED AND MOCKED: MARK 15:1-5, 15-20

Artist statement: "From the Ashes"

I wanted to emphasize Jesus' solidarity with the despised, afflicted, and rejected, as well as communicate his silent strength and confidence before his accusers. This piece incorporates ashes I collected after burning a list of painful accusations levied against me. What ashes of judgment or condemnation would you contribute to the painting? What does the despised, afflicted, and rejected One communicate to you today?

As soon as it was morning, the chief priests held a consultation with the elders and scribes and the whole council. They bound Jesus, led him away, and handed him over to Pilate. Pilate asked him, "Are you the King of the Jews?" He answered him, "You say so." Then the chief priests accused him of many things. Pilate asked him again, "Have you no answer? See how many charges they bring against you." But Jesus made no further reply, so that Pilate was amazed . . .

So Pilate, wishing to satisfy the crowd, released Barabbas for them; and after flogging Jesus, he handed him over to be crucified. Then the soldiers led him into the courtyard of the palace (that is, the governor's headquarters); and they called together the whole cohort. And they clothed him in a purple cloak; and after twisting some thorns into a crown, they put it on him. And they began saluting him, "Hail, King of the Jews!" They struck his head with a reed, spat upon him, and knelt down in homage to him. After mocking him, they stripped him of the purple cloak and put his own clothes on him. Then they led him out to crucify him. (Mark 15:1-5, 15-20)

- ▶ Pilate is amazed by Jesus' refusal to answer the accusations hurled at him. Imagine you are there, watching Jesus remain silent. How do you respond? What would you like to say to Jesus?

  - What would you like to say to Pilate and the others?

- ▶ What is your response when you are accused?

  - How does Jesus' example speak to you?

▶ Peter writes, "When he was abused, he did not return abuse; when he suffered, he did not threaten; but he entrusted himself to the one who judges justly" (1 Peter 2:23). The word for "entrusted" in 1 Peter 2:23 is from the verb *paradidomi*. Even as Jesus was "handed over" to the authorities, Jesus "handed himself over" to God with deep trust. What helps you "hand yourself over" to God?

- What hinders you?

▶ Speak with God about what you have noticed during your time of reflection.

STATION FIVE
JESUS SPEAKS TO THE WOMEN OF JERUSALEM: LUKE 23:27-31

Artist statement: "Lament"

For this station we offer not only our sorrow but also our longings and hopes, not just for ourselves but also for the world. What images capture the heart of your lament? Why? What does it mean for you to fasten these to the cross? How does the layering of your lament with the laments of others speak to you?

A great number of the people followed him, and among them were women who were beating their breasts and wailing for him. But Jesus turned to them and said, "Daughters of Jerusalem, do not weep for me, but weep for yourselves and for your children. For the days are surely coming when they will say, 'Blessed are the barren, and the wombs that never bore, and the breasts that never nursed.' Then they will begin to say to the mountains, 'Fall on us'; and to the hills, 'Cover us.' For if they do this when the wood is green, what will happen when it is dry?" (Luke 23:27-31)

- ▶ Imagine you are following Jesus on the way to the cross. What are your thoughts and emotions as you walk with him?
- ▶ What do you want to say to him?
- ▶ What do you long for him to say to you?
- ▶ What causes you to weep? Why?
  - How readily do you lament for those you know?
    - For strangers?
    - For yourself?
- ▶ Is Jesus calling you to weep for anyone today? If so, whom?
- ▶ What does it mean for you to keep company with the Man of Sorrows, acquainted with grief?
  - In what sorrows does Jesus keep you company today?
- ▶ Speak with God about what you have noticed during your time of reflection.

STATION SIX
JESUS IS CRUCIFIED: LUKE 23:32-43

Artist statement: "Remember Me"

Just as the thief on the cross said to Jesus, "Remember me," so too Jesus says to us, "Remember me." What does it look like to be broken and poured out in self-giving love for others? The bread and the cup remind us of Jesus' sacrifice and call us to participate in sharing his life and presence with our broken world. What do you need to remember today? How will you practice remembering him?

Two others also, who were criminals, were led away to be put to death with him. When they came to the place that is called The Skull, they crucified Jesus there with the criminals, one on his right and one on his left. Then Jesus said, "Father, forgive them; for they do not know what they are doing." And they cast lots to divide his clothing. And the people stood by, watching; but the leaders scoffed at him, saying, "He saved others; let him save himself if he is the Messiah of God, his chosen one!" The soldiers also mocked him, coming up and offering him sour wine, and saying, "If you are the King of the Jews, save yourself!" There was also an inscription over him, "This is the King of the Jews."

One of the criminals who were hanged there kept deriding him and saying, "Are you not the Messiah? Save yourself and us!" But the other rebuked him, saying, "Do you not fear God, since you are under the same sentence of condemnation? And we indeed have been condemned justly, for we are getting what we deserve for our deeds, but this man has done nothing wrong." Then he said, "Jesus, remember me when you come into your kingdom." He replied, "Truly I tell you, today you will be with me in Paradise." (Luke 23:32-43)

- ▶ Imagine you are at the foot of the cross, watching and listening to everything unfold. What thoughts, memories, or emotions are stirred in you?

  - Do you keep silent, or do you speak? If you speak, what do you say?

- ▶ Picture yourself as one of the criminals next to Jesus. What do you say to him? Why?
  - What do you want him to do?
- ▶ Which words, action, or inaction of Jesus speak most loudly to you? Why?
- ▶ Speak with God about what you have noticed during your time of reflection.

STATION SEVEN
JESUS SPEAKS AGAIN FROM THE CROSS: JOHN 19:25-27

Artist statement: "Hope Rises"

Before he dies, Jesus speaks words of love to his mother and beloved friend, entrusting them to one another. While witnesses gather at the foot of the cross, creation also testifies to the suffering and sacrifice of Jesus as darkness presses in to cover the whole land. But the true light shines in the darkness, and the darkness will not overcome it. What messengers and evidence of hope do you perceive in the landscape of your life?

Meanwhile, standing near the cross of Jesus were his mother, and his mother's sister, Mary the wife of Clopas, and Mary Magdalene. When Jesus saw his mother and the disciple whom he loved standing beside her, he said to his mother, "Woman, here is your son." Then he said to the disciple, "Here is your mother." And from that hour the disciple took her into his own home. (John 19:25-27)

▶ What catches your attention about the words Jesus speaks to his mother and his disciple? Why?

▶ Picture yourself at the foot of the cross, looking up at Jesus. He is bruised and bleeding. His breath is labored. You have no power to intervene, and he is doing nothing to resist evil. What do you want to say to him?

▶ Imagine Jesus looking down and seeing that you are there, standing with him. His eyes light up with love, and he opens his mouth to speak to you. How do you feel?

  • What do you hope Jesus will say to you?

▶ Imagine you are nearing the end of your life. Which people do you hope will surround you?

  • What requests would you make of them? Why?

▶ What last words would you like to speak to loved ones?

  • What last words would you like loved ones to speak to you?

  • What important conversations could you have with one another now?

▶ Speak with God about what you have noticed during your time of reflection.

STATION EIGHT
JESUS DIES ON THE CROSS: JOHN 19:28-30

Artist statement: "It Is Finished" (B. L. Dickinson)

Set over the backdrop of the cosmos, Christ is represented here in a posture of both dying and rising over all things. It is through both the crucifixion and resurrection that he brings unity and fulfillment to all things in heaven and earth. The cross and empty tomb cannot be separated. In Christ, where you find death, so also you find life. Where you find darkness, there is also light. He invites us into the experience of both in order to make us whole in him.

After this, when Jesus knew that all was now finished, he said (in order to fulfill the scripture), "I am thirsty." A jar full of sour wine was standing there. So they put a sponge full of the wine on a branch of hyssop and held it to his mouth. When Jesus had received the wine, he said, "It is finished." Then he bowed his head and gave up his spirit. (John 19:28-30)

▶ Imagine you are at the foot of the cross, watching these final moments of Jesus' earthly life unfold. What thoughts, memories, or emotions are stirred in you as you hear him express his thirst and as you watch them lift a sponge full of sour wine to his parched lips?

• What would you like to do for him or say to him?

▶ Hear Jesus speak the words, "It is finished." With what tone of voice do you hear him say this?

• What do these words mean to you?

▶ Ponder the words, "gave up his spirit." What does this final act signify to you?

▶ Speak with God about what you have noticed during your time of reflection.

Acknowledgments

I am profoundly grateful to artist and teacher Elizabeth Ivy Hawkins for saying yes to painting as Wren Crawford. It's challenging enough to paint with your own voice and in your own style—but to inhabit a fictional character whose style, passions, and limitations as an amateur had already been established in *Shades of Light* required a particular brand of courage and skill. Not only did Elizabeth take to heart Wren's temperament and fears, but she also leaned into Wren's creativity and spirituality. It was a joy to work with Elizabeth on this project, and I'm grateful for her attentive receptivity to the Spirit's guidance and inspiration. I hope you'll visit her website (www.elizabethivy.com) to purchase prints, explore her other work, and learn more about art as a spiritual practice.

I'm also grateful to my friend Bette Lynn Dickinson (www .bettedickinson.life), who generously gave permission for me to use the center panel of her larger work titled, "What Breathes Beneath Our Story" as the art for station eight. Bette is a gifted artist and ministry leader who uses art to facilitate encounters with God. Prints of all her paintings are available on her website.

To Therese Kay (www.theresekayphotography.com), Jennifer Oosterhouse, and Martie Bradley, who shared photos for the prayer collage, thank you!

To the stellar team at IVP and especially to my editor, Cindy Bunch, and my marketer, Lori Neff, who were with me at dinner when the complex vision for this book began to emerge. Thank you for journeying with me through all the "what if" possibilities for this work. Thanks, too, to Jeanna Wiggins for the beautiful interior design and to Elissa Schauer for her excellence in managing all the details of production. Jeff Crosby, you are a gifted leader and a kind and generous friend. Thank you.

To my prayer partners, friends, and family: I couldn't do any of this without your love and support. You share in this ministry with me, and I am deeply grateful. Mom and Beth, we share the grief and also the hope of resurrection as we remember Dad together and celebrate the beauty and faithfulness of his life. I love you and am so grateful God gave me the gift of each of you. Jack and David, though it's my name on the cover, your wisdom and compassion fill the pages. I love you and thank God for you.

Finally, to you, Lord. All of this is from you, through you, and for you. To you be the glory. Always.

Also Available

Shades of Light
978-0-8308-4658-0

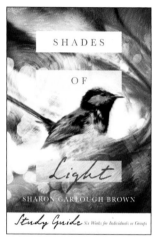

Shades of Light Study Guide
978-0-8308-4664-1

Shades of Light Audiobook
978-0-8308-4667-2

Visit sharongarloughbrown.com *for book club resources*

The Sensible Shoes Series

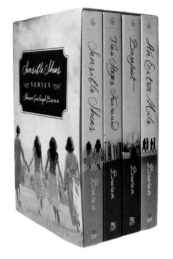

Sensible Shoes
Two Steps Forward
Barefoot
An Extra Mile